Crossings

ILLINOIS SHORT FICTION

CROSSINGS

Stories by Stephen Minot

UNIVERSITY OF ILLINOIS PRESS

Urbana   Chicago   London

Manufactured in the United States of America

"Sausage and Beer," an "Atlantic First," *Atlantic Monthly*, November, 1962; included in *The Story*, ed. Mark Schorer (Prentice-Hall), and in *Three Genres*, Stephen Minot (Prentice-Hall).

"Small Point Bridge," *Virginia Quarterly Review*, Winter, 1969; included in *Journeys: An Introduction to Literature*, ed. Larry M. Sutton et al. (Holbrook).

"Windy Fourth," appeared as "Windy 4th," *Virginia Quarterly Review*, Winter, 1964.

"The Tide and Isaac Bates," *The Quarterly Review of Literature*, Summer, 1973; selected for the Martha Foley collection, *The Best American Short Stories, 1974*.

"Grubbing for Roots," *North American Review*, Spring, 1975.

"Bruno in the Hall of Mirrors," *North American Review*, Spring, 1970.

"Greek Mysteries," appeared as "Prodigal's Father," *Carleton Miscellany*, Spring, 1968.

"I Remember the Day God Died Like It Was Yesterday," *Carleton Miscellany*, Spring, 1966.

"Crossings," *Redbook*, February, 1967; presented as a dramatic reading at the Image Theater, Hartford, Conn., March, 1967.

"Teddy, Where Are You?" *The Ladies' Home Journal*, September, 1968; reprinted in *Woman's Own* (England), 1969.

"Mars Revisited," *Virginia Quarterly Review*, Spring, 1970; selected for *O. Henry Prize Stories, 1971*; included in *Mirrors: An Introduction to Literature*, J. R. Knott & C. R. Reaske (Canfield Press).

"Estuaries," *Virginia Quarterly Review*, Winter, 1974.

Library of Congress Cataloging in Publication Data

Minot, Stephen.
  Crossings.

  (Illinois short fiction)
  CONTENTS: Sausage and beer.—Small point bridge.—
Windy Fourth. [etc.]
  I. Title.
PZ4.M665Cr   [PS3563.I475]   813'.5'4   74-14915
ISBN 0-252-00530-9
ISBN 0-252-00472-8 pbk.

For Reid, Nick, and Chris

Contents

Sausage and Beer

I kept quiet for most of the trip. It was too cold for talk. The car, a 1929 Dodge, was still fairly new, but it had no heater, and I knew from experience that no matter how carefully I tucked the black bearskin robe about me, the cold would seep through the door cracks and, starting with a dull ache in my ankles, would work up my legs. There was nothing to do but sit still and wonder what Uncle Theodore would be like.

"Is it very far?" I asked at last. My words puffed vapor.

"We're about halfway now," he said.

That was all. Not enough, of course, but I hadn't expected much more. My father kept to his own world, and he didn't invite children to share it. Nor did he impose himself on us. My twin sister and I were allowed to live our own lives, and our parents led theirs, and there was a mutual respect for the border. In fact, when we were younger Tina and I had assumed that we would eventually marry each other, and while those plans were soon revised, the family continued to exist as two distinct couples.

But this particular January day was different, because Tina hadn't been invited—nor had Mother. I was twelve that winter, and I believe it was the first time I had ever gone anywhere alone with my father.

The whole business of visiting Uncle Theodore had come up in the most unconvincingly offhand manner.

"Thought I'd visit your Uncle Theodore," he had said that day after Sunday dinner. "Wondered if you'd like to meet him."

He spoke with his eyes on a crack in the ceiling as if the idea had just popped into his head, but that didn't fool me. It was quite obvious that he had waited until both Tina and my mother were in the kitchen washing the dishes, that he had rehearsed it, and that I wasn't really being given a choice.

"Is Tina going?" I asked.

"No, she isn't feeling well."

I knew what that meant. But I also knew that my father was just using it as an excuse. So I got my coat.

The name Uncle Theodore had a familiar ring, but it was just a name. And I had learned early that you do not ask about relatives who don't come up in adult conversation naturally. At least, you didn't in my family. You can never tell— Like my Uncle Harry. He was another one of my father's brothers. My parents never said anything about Uncle Harry, but some of my best friends at school told me he'd taken a big nail, a spike really, and driven it into his heart with a ball peen hammer. I didn't believe it, so they took me to the library and we found the article on the front page of the *Herald* for the previous Saturday, so it must have been true.

I thought a lot about that. It seemed to me that a grown-up ought to be able to *shove* it between his ribs. And even if he couldn't, what was the point of the ball peen hammer? I used to put myself to sleep feeling the soft spaces between my ribs and wondering just which one was directly over my heart.

But no one at school told me about Uncle Theodore, because they didn't know he existed. Even I hadn't any real proof until that day. I knew that my father had a brother named Theodore, in the same way I knew the earth was round without anyone ever taking me to the library to prove it. But then, there were many brothers I had never met—like Freddie, who had joined a Theosophist colony somewhere in California and wore robes like a priest, and Uncle Herb, who was once in jail for leading a strike in New York, or Uncle Ike, who was a fisherman with lots of children in Maine.

We were well out in the New England countryside now, passing dark, snow-patched farm fields and scrubby woodlands where saplings choked and stunted each other. I tried to visualize this Uncle Theodore as a farmer: blue overalls, straw hat, chewing a long stem of alfalfa, and misquoting the Bible. But it was a highly unsatisfactory conjecture. Next I tried to conjure up a mystic living in—didn't St. Francis live in a cave? But it wasn't the sort of question I could ask my father. All I had to go on was what he had told me, which was nothing. And I knew without thinking that he didn't want me to ask him directly.

After a while I indulged in my old trick of fixing my eyes on the big radiator thermometer mounted like a figurehead on the front end of the hood. If you do that long enough the blur of the road just beyond will lull you nicely and pass the time. It had begun to take effect when I felt the car slow down and turn abruptly. Two great gates flashed by, and we were inside a kind of walled city.

Prison, I thought. That's it. That's why they kept him quiet. A murderer, maybe. "My Uncle Theodore," I rehearsed silently, "he's the cop killer."

The place went on forever, row after row of identical buildings, four stories, brick, slate roofs, narrow windows with wire mesh. There wasn't a bright color anywhere. The brick had aged to gray, and so had the snow patches along the road. We passed a group of three old men lethargically shoveling ice and crusted snow into a two-wheeled horse cart; men and horse were the same hue. It was the sort of setting you have in dreams which are not nightmares but still manage to leave a clinging aftertaste. At least, *I* have dreams like that.

"This is a kind of hospital," my father said flatly as we drove between the staring brick fronts. There was a slow whine to second gear which sang harmony to something in me. I had based my courage on the romance of a prison, but even this slim hold on assurance was lost with the word "hospital."

"It's big," I said.

"It's enormous," he said, and then turned his whole attention to studying the numbers over each door. There was something in his tone that suggested that he didn't like the place either, and that did a lot to sustain me.

Uncle Theodore's building was 13-M, but aside from the number, it resembled the others. The door had been painted a dark green for many years, and the layers of paint over chipped and blistered paint gave it a mottled look. We had to wait quite a while before someone responded to the push bell.

A man let us in, not a nurse. And the man was clearly no doctor either. He wore a gray shirt which was clean but unpressed, and dark green work pants with a huge ring of keys hanging from his belt. But for the keys he might have been a W.P.A. worker.

"Hello there, Mr. Bates," he said in a round Irish voice to match his round face. "You brought the boy?"

"I brought the boy." My father's voice was reedy by comparison. "How's Ted?"

"Same as when you called. A little gloomy, maybe, but calm. Those boils have just about gone."

"Good," my father said.

"Funny about those boils. I don't remember a year but what he's had trouble. Funny."

My father agreed it was funny, and then we went into the visiting room to await Uncle Theodore.

The room was large, and it seemed even larger for the lack of furniture. There were benches around all four walls, and in the middle there was a long table flanked with two more benches. The rest was space. And through that space old men shuffled, younger men wheeled carts of linen, a woman visitor walked slowly up and down with her restless husband—or brother, or uncle. Or was she the patient? I couldn't decide which might be the face of madness, his troubled and shifting eyes or her deadened look. Beyond, a bleak couple counseled an ancient patient. I strained to hear, wanting to know the language of the place, but I could only make out mumbles.

The smell was oddly familiar. I cast about; this was no home smell. And then I remembered trips with my mother to a place called the Refuge, where the lucky brought old clothes, old furniture, old magazines, and old kitchenware to be bought by the unlucky. My training in Christian charity was to bring my chipped and dented toys and dump them into a great bin, where they were pored over by dead-faced mothers and children.

"Smells like the Refuge," I said very softly, not wanting to hurt anyone's feelings. My father nodded with an almost smile.

We went over to the corner where the benches met, though there was space to sit almost anywhere. And there we waited.

A couple of times I glanced cautiously at my father's face, hoping for some sort of guide. He could have been waiting for a train or listening to a sermon, and I felt a surge of respect. He had a long face with a nose so straight it looked as if it had been leveled with a rule. I guess he would have been handsome if he hadn't seemed so sad or tired much of the time. He worked for a paint wholesaler which had big, dusty offices in a commercial section of Dorchester. When I was younger I used to think the dirt of that place had rubbed off on him permanently. But later I could see that it wasn't just the job, it was home too. The place had been built in the eighties, the pride of our grandfather. But it was no pride to us. It was a gross Victorian imitation in brick of the square sea captain's house, complete with two iron deer on the lawn. At some point the brick had been painted a mournful gray. It was lucky, our parents kept telling each other, that grandfather never lived to see what happened to the place. The land was sold off bit by bit, and the city of Dorchester, once a kind of rural cousin to Boston, spread slowly the way tide comes in over mud flats, until it surrounded us with little brick stores—hardware, drug, delicatessen, plumbing—on one side and double-deckers on the other three. Somehow my father had come to feel responsible for all this; it was his nature to take on more responsibility than most people do.

For Tina and me the place had its compensations. We called it the Ark, and we knew every level of that enormous place, from the kitchen with its cook's pantry without a cook and a maid's pantry without a maid up through the four floors to the glass-sided cupola which we called the Bridge and reserved as our private area, just as our parents reserved their bedroom.

We used to arrange the future from up there; I the father and she the mother, planning on two children—twins, of course. And we also planned to replace the iron deer with live ones, paint the Ark a shimmering green, and burn down Gemini's Delicatessen across the street—the one with sausages hanging in the window—because Mother had told us that it was just a front for the numbers racket which kept customers streaming through the doors. She detested sausage and resented having the numbers game played "at our very door," so, naturally, in the name of order it had to go.

But waiting for Uncle Theodore in that dream room was worlds away from all that youthful planning. I could see, or thought I saw, in my father's face a kind of resignation which I used to interpret as fatigue but now felt was his true strength.

I began to study the patients with the hope of preparing myself for Uncle Theodore. The old man beside us was stretched out on the bench full length, feet toward us, one arm over his eyes, as if he were lying on the beach, the other resting over his crotch. He had a kind of squeak to his snore. There was nothing in him I could not accept as my Uncle Theodore. Another patient was persistently scratching his back on the dark-varnished door frame. If this were Uncle Theodore, I wondered, would I be expected to scratch his back for him? It wasn't a very rational speculation, but there was nothing about the place that encouraged clear reasoning.

Then my father stood up, and when I did too, I could see that Uncle Theodore was being led in by a Negro who wore the same kind of key ring at his waist that the Irishman had. The Negro nodded to my father, pointing him out to Uncle Theodore, and then set him free with a little nudge as if he were about to pin the tail on the donkey.

Surprisingly, Uncle Theodore was heavy. I don't mean fat, because he wasn't solid. He was a great, sagging man. His jowls hung loose, his shoulders were massive but rounded like a dome, his hands were attached like brass weights on the ends of swinging pendulums. He wore a clean white shirt open at the neck and blue serge suit pants hung on suspenders which had been patched with a length of twine. It looked as if his pants had once been five sizes too large and that somehow, with the infinite patience of the infirm, he had managed to stretch the lower half of his stomach to fill them.

I would have assumed that he was far older than my father from his stance and his shuffling walk (he wore scuffs, which he slid across the floor without once lifting them), but his face was a baby pink, which made him look adolescent.

"Hello, Ted," my father said. "How have you been?"

Uncle Theodore just said "Hello," without a touch of enthusiasm, or even gratitude for our coming to see him. We stood there, the three of us, for an awkward moment.

Then: "I brought the boy."

"Who?"

"My boy, Will."

Uncle Theodore looked down at me with red-rimmed blue eyes. Then he looked at my father, puzzled. "But *you're* Will."

"Right, but we've named our boy William too. Tried to call him Billy, but he insists on Will. Very confusing."

Uncle Theodore smiled for the first time. The smile made everything much easier; I relaxed. He was going to be like any other relative on a Sunday afternoon visit.

"Well, now," he said in an almost jovial manner, "there's one on me. I'd forgotten I even *had* a boy."

My face tingled the way it does when you open the furnace door. Somehow he had joined himself with my father as a married couple, and done it with a smile. No instruction could have prepared me for this quiet sound of madness.

But my father had, it seemed, learned how to handle it. He simply asked Uncle Theodore if he had enjoyed the magazines he had brought last time. We subscribed to the old version of *Life*, and my mother used to buy *Judge* on the newsstand fairly regularly. It was the right subject to bring up, because Uncle Theodore promptly forgot about who had produced what child and told us about how all his copies of *Life* had been stolen. He even pointed out the thief.

"The little one with the hook nose there," he said with irritation but no rage. "Stuffs them in his pants to make him look bigger. He's a problem, he is."

"I'll send you more," my father said. "Perhaps the attendant will keep them for you."

"Hennesy? He's a good one. Plays checkers like a pro."

"I'll bet he has a hard time beating you."

"Hasn't yet. Not once."

"I'm not surprised. You were always the winner." And then to me: "We used to play up in the cupola for hours at a stretch."

This jolted me. It hadn't occurred to me that the two of them had spent a childhood together. I even let some of their conversation slip by thinking of how they had grown up in the Ark, had discovered the Bridge before I was born, had perhaps planned the future while sitting up there, looking down on the world, on Gemini's Delicatessen and all the other little stores, had gone to school together, and then at some point— But what point? And how? It was as incomprehensible to me looking back as it must have been for them looking forward.

"So they started banging on their plates," Uncle Theodore was saying, "and shouting for more heat. Those metal plates sure make a racket, I can tell you."

"That's no way to get heat," Father said, sounding paternal.

"Guess not. They put Schwartz and Cooper in the pit. That's what Hennesy said. And there's a bunch of them that's gone to different levels. They send them down when they act like that, you know. The doctors, they take a vote and send the troublemakers down." And then his voice lowered. Instinctively we both bent toward him for some confidence. "And I've found out—God's truth—that one of these nights they're going to shut down the heat *all the way. Freeze us!"*

There was a touch of panic in this which coursed through me. I could feel just how it would be, this great room black as midnight, the whine of wind outside, and then all those hissing radiators turning silent, and the aching cold seeping through the door cracks—

"Nonsense," my father said quietly, and I knew at once that it was nonsense. "They wouldn't do that. Hennesy's a friend of mine. I'll speak to him before I go."

"You do that," Uncle Theodore said with genuine gratitude, putting his hand on my father's knee. "You do that for us. I don't believe there would be a soul of us"—he swept his hand about expansively—"not a soul of us alive if it weren't for your influence."

My father nodded and then turned the conversation to milder topics. He talked about how the sills were rotting under the house, how a neighborhood gang had broken two windows one night, how there was talk of replacing the trolley with a bus line, how Imperial Paint, where my father worked, had laid off fifty percent of it employees, how business was so bad it couldn't get worse. But Uncle Theodore didn't seem very concerned. He was much more bothered about how a man named Altman was losing his eyesight because of the steam heat and how stern and unfair Hennesy was. At one point he moved back in time to describe a fishing trip by canoe through the Rangeley Lakes. It was like opening a great window, flooding the place with light and color and the smells of summer.

Nothing finer," he said, his eyes half shut, "than frying those trout at the end of the day with the water so still you'd think you could walk on it."

He was interrupted by the sleeper on the bench beside us, who woke, stood, and stared down at us. Uncle Theodore told him to "Go blow," and when he had gone so were the Rangeley Lakes.

"Rangeley?" he asked, when my father tried to open that window again by suggestion. "He must be one of our cousins. Can't keep 'em straight." And we were back to Mr. Altman's deafness and how seriously it hindered him and how the doctors paid no attention.

It was with relief that I smelled sauerkraut. That plus attendants gliding through with carts of food in dented steel containers seemed to suggest supper, and supper promised that the end was near.

"About suppertime," my father said after a particularly long silence.

Uncle Theodore took in a long, deep breath. He held it for a moment. Then he let it go with the slowest, saddest sigh I have ever heard.

"About suppertime," he said at the end of it.

There were mumbled farewells and nods of agreement. We were thanked for copies of *Judge* which we hadn't brought; he was told he was looking fine, just fine.

We were only inches from escape when Uncle Theodore suddenly discovered me again.

"Tell me, son," he said, bending down with a smile which on anyone else would have been friendly, "what d'you think of your Uncle Ted?"

I was overwhelmed. I stood there looking up at him, waiting for my father to save me. But he said nothing.

"It's been very nice meeting you," I said to the frozen pink smile, dredging the phrase up from my sparse catechism of social responses, assuming that what would do for maiden aunts would do for Uncle Theodore.

But it did not. He laughed. It was a loud and bitter laugh, derisive, and perfectly sane. He had seen my statement for the lie it was, had caught sight of himself, of all of us.

"Well," he said when the laugh withered, "say hi to Dad for me. Tell him to drop by."

Father said he would, and we left, grateful that the moment of sanity had been so brief.

It was dark when we got back into the car, and it was just beginning to snow. I nestled into the seat, soothed by the familiar whine of second gear.

We had been on the road about a half hour when my father said quite abruptly, "I could do with a drink." It was so spontaneous, so perfectly confidential that I wanted to reply, to keep some sort of exchange going. But I couldn't suggest a place to go—I couldn't even throw back an easy "So could I."

"It's OK with me," I said, without any of the casual air I tried hard to achieve.

There was a long pause. He flipped the manual windshield wiper. Then he said, "I don't suppose you like sausage."

"I love sausage," I said, though I had never had any at home.

"Well," he said slowly, "There's a place I go—but it might be better to tell your mother we went to a Dutchland Farms for supper."

"Sure," I said, and reached up to flip the windshield wiper for him.

When we got to the city we traveled on roads I had never been on. He finally parked on a dark street and began what turned out to be a three-block hike. It ended at an unlit door, and after some mumbled consultations through an apartment phone we were ushered into a warm, bubbling, sparkling, humming, soothing, exciting bit of cheerful chaos. There was a bar to our right, marble tables ahead, booths beyond, just as I had pictured from the cartoons in *Life* magazine. My father nodded at a waiter and said hi to a group at a table, then headed toward the booths with a sure step.

We hadn't got halfway before a fat man in a double-breasted suit came steaming up to us, furious.

"Whatcha doing," he said even before he reached us, "corruptin' the youth?"

I held my breath. But when the big man reached my father they broke out in easy laughter.

"So this is the boy?" he said. "Will, Junior—right?" We nodded. "Well, there's a good part of you in the boy, I can see that—it's in the eyes. Now, there's a girl too, isn't there? Younger?"

"She's my twin," I said. "Not identical."

The men laughed. Then the fat one said, "Jesus, twins sure run in your family, don't they!"

This surprised me. I knew of no other twins except some cousins from Maine. I looked up at my father, puzzled.

"Me and Ted," he said to me. "We're twins. Nonidentical."

We were ushered to a booth, and the fat man hovered over us, waiting for the order.

"Got sausage tonight?" my father asked.

"Sure. American or some nice hot Italian?"

"Italian."

"Drinks?"

"Well—" My father turned to me. "I guess you rate beer," he said. And then, to the fat man, "Two beers."

The man relayed the order to a passing waiter. Then he asked my father, "Been out to see Ted?"

"You guessed it."

"I figured." He paused, his smile gone. "You too?" he asked me.

"Yes," I said. "It was my first time."

"Oh," he said, with a series of silent nods which assured me that somehow he knew exactly what my afternoon had been like. "Ted was quite a boy. A great tackle. A pleasure to watch him. But no dope either. Used to win meals here playing chess. Never saw him lose. Why, he sat right over there."

He pointed to the corner booth, which had a round table. All three of us looked; a waiter with a tray full of dirty glasses stopped, turned, and also looked at the empty booth as if an apparition had just been sighted.

"And you know why he's locked up?"

"No," I whispered, appalled at the question.

"It's just the number he drew. Simple as that. Your Dad, me, you—any of us could draw the wrong number tomorrow. There's something to think about."

I nodded. All three of us nodded. Then the waiter brought a tray with the order, and the fat man left us with a quick, benedictory smile. We ate and drank quietly, lost in a kind of communion.

Small Point Bridge

It was March 31 and Isaac Bates had survived still another Maine winter. Now, his solitary lunch finished, he stood for a moment by the large living room window and looked down over the white stubble of glazed brush, farther down to the ledges along the shore and out to the churning sea, and enjoyed his one cigar for the day. He also savored their consternation: sons and daughters in Connecticut, Tennessee, California, and all over, neighbors back on the town road, all amazed that a man of his age who could easily afford to live anywhere would stick it out for the length of another winter. He had been snowed in for two months and three days. The old dirt road between his place and the highway was too steep for truck or tractor plowing; and even now, with the partial thaw, it was only fit for Jeep travel. There weren't many who would put up with all of that.

"No *sir*," he said aloud.

It hadn't been easy. It never was, of course, but this year the snows had come early and the oil truck couldn't make a December delivery so by January he was using the kerosene space heater and by February he was back to coal in the cookstove and wood in the fireplaces. The children were forever writing him to get out of there; but what the hell, generations had lived in that house on the heat of good oak firewood. Better for you anyway. Oil heat cakes the lungs.

So now he was almost up to another April. During the dark

months he'd told himself that if he stuck it to April he'd last another year and, as he told the children, a man past seventy bargains for short-term leases. The low point had come when the pipes froze and he had to shut off the water. That meant shoveling a path to the outhouse. In the old days he and the boys kept that path open morning by morning, which was easier in the long run than cutting through three months' accumulation. . . . Well, that was all behind him now.

But the winter wasn't through yet. There was still a kick to it. A March gale had begun the previous day and had built up strong during the night. Now, spitting sleet and rain, it churned the bay into an ugly froth. Only a month ago the ice had been thick enough for deer to wander out to the islands, and one young fool had driven his Ford pick-up out past Peniel Island just for the dare of it. But now the gale had broken that white valley up into slabs of forty and fifty tons and was grinding them against the shore. Tide and wind had jacked them up into weird angles like a nightmare of train wrecks. But unlike boxcars, they were forever moving—slow as a clock's hand and with a force you could hardly believe.

There was one year when the ice had caught hold of the marine railway he used to haul his fishing boats. Within an agonizing week it had pried those railroad tracks from the ties spike by spike and had slowly twisted them into hairpin shapes. The memory of it made him grimace even now.

From where he stood in his living room he could hear the inhuman whine and grunt as ice heaved blindly against ledge. The sound had been loud enough to pry its way into his dreams the night before.

"Snarl all you want," he muttered and blew cigar smoke against the window where it broke like surf. "You can't move granite." His shore line was solid ledge, and there was satisfaction in that. It was solid like his house, like the plate glass that stood between him and the driving sleet—he had seen full-grown pheasants break their necks against that glass.

The storm would do damage at the cannery. He knew that. He had seen the ice lock onto the base of a pile two feet thick and work it back and forth with the incoming tide, pulling it clear out of the muck and lifting the pier above it as well. He'd seen the oak hull of a lobster boat crushed like a beer can in a young man's grip. No sir, he wouldn't get by a winter like this without getting hurt somewhere. But there was money for repairs. In half a century he had built his cannery with solid blocks of effort: first, fresh crabmeat for the summer hotels; then canned crabmeat statewide; finally frozen seafood of all types coast to coast. As his billboards said, "You Can't Beat Bates for Frozen Fishcakes." And no one had. No matter what they threw at him, there was always the satisfaction that he had insured himself with bank accounts. "There's more than one way to build a sea wall," he said, and nodded, serving as his own audience.

But he was talking to himself again. That wasn't good. It meant he was getting weak-headed. "Keep your mouth shut," he said. What he needed was a little activity.

Then he remembered that this was the 31st. This was the day he had to see Seth. He probably should have taken care of it before this, but now they were at the deadline. And he had almost forgotten it.

It was a small business matter and Seth would be surprised that such details are important—Seth being a simple man. But a debt's a debt and all the world knew that. If you let the little things go—well, it's like not tending to a small leak.

"Rotten day to be out," he said, but he felt no deep resentment. He never expected the weather to give him an even break.

He went to the front hall and began burrowing in the cluttered closet. "Where's those boots?" he muttered. "Damn it, Ella, where's those boots?" Then he clamped his jaw on his cigar, cursing himself silently. Ella was dead—dead, buried, and gone two years now. It was weak-headed to call her name. Besides, it wouldn't do to let her know he was still living here. "Promise," she had said, looking up at him from that ugly hospital bed, and he had promised: he would move out of the old place when she was gone. And he would, too—when the time came to join her.

"Where the hell. . .?" And he spotted his boots just where he had left them on the chair—together with his coat, his lumberman's cap, his tool box, his axe, his snow shovel, the broken car jack, his extra set of chains, and an empty anti-freeze can. Of course. "Got to clean up this goddamn mess," he said with the tone he used to use on the children.

The old barn was dank and colder than the outside air; but for all this his Jeep started easily enough. During the winter months Isaac had run the motor for an hour each week with religious regularity; that, plus the recent trips to the store, had left the battery charged. All it took was a little foresight.

He backed out and drove past the barn through the apple orchards and down into the spruce grove. At the bottom of the ravine by the brook he stopped and shifted into four-wheel drive. The long, twisting ascent was a brutal challenge. It took two wild runs, wheels whining and spewing half-frozen cakes of mud; but he made it, finally, with a grunt of satisfaction.

"Crazy road," he muttered to himself, as he had said to every visitor who had ever come over it. It was the only route out from the farm to the highway and thus the only link with the store, with the town, and even with his cannery. He had cursed it and repaired it every spring; but it had its uses. It moved the assessors to pity, kept salesmen out, turned back summer tourists, and intimidated talkative neighbors. There was no gate or sign that could do all that.

Once on the tar road, he made good time. He had to dodge fallen branches and allow for sleet on the pavement, but it was not long before he came to the turn which led back onto his own acreage again, back down to the sea again where his cannery stood gray and silent on ice-caked piles, dormant and waiting like his orchard.

Small Point Road ran parallel to the sea from the cannery to Seth's place, less than a quarter-mile. It was a godforsaken bit of coastline with a few unpainted houses, a dump, and only scrub oak and choke cherry for coverage.

Isaac owned that entire section of the coast including Small Point itself, a useless nob of land cut off from the shore by muck at low tide and six feet of water at high. Seth had built his house out there with permission. It was made from driftwood and used lumber collected over the years he had spent working at the cannery. It didn't look like much—just a wood-shingled shack actually—but you could see it was put together with care. None of the windows matched, for example, but they were well fitted and puttied and not a cracked pane in the lot.

He had also built the ramshackle footbridge which led out to the house. As Isaac started to walk across it he could feel the ice heave against the untrimmed spruce piling. The cold wind seared his lungs and made his eyes tear and he wondered what drove a man to live like this. He hung on to the railing as if it were a lifeline and watched his footing carefully. Sections of the footbridge were already out of alignment, leaving gaps and twisting the planks.

"Goddamned thing ought to be condemned," Isaac muttered. But he forgot all that when his feet touched solid ground again. "Ah!" he said, and headed for the shack.

Seth opened the door even before the knock. His eyesight had grown poor and at first he only squinted, not recognizing Isaac. Then he nodded as if he had known all along. Isaac stepped in quickly and shut the door against the wind.

"Just having breakfast," Seth said. As night watchman, his day began in the afternoon. He was a short man and stooped, so he had to peer up at Isaac when he spoke. "Got some hot coffee going."

"It'll take more than coffee," Isaac said, struggling with his boots.

"I've got some of that too."

"Just a thimble, Seth. Can't stay long."

It was a one-room place, furnished only with necessities: wood stove, kitchen table, two straight chairs, and a bunk of two-by-fours built against the wall. Along the opposite wall were hooks on which his clothes and foul-weather gear were hung neatly. It was all snug enough until you looked out the front window and saw the ominous blocks of ice shoved in a jumble up the ledge to within twenty feet of the house.

Seth poured coffee from the percolator on the stove and then got a fifth of King's Whiskey from a cupboard and added a liberal jigger. They sat down at the table.

"Hasn't let up much," Isaac said.

"She's got another night to run."

"Bad time for it," Isaac said. "One more week and we'd be free of that ice." They nodded. "That bridge of yours has heaved a bit."

"Always does."

"I don't suppose you'd consider staying ashore till this ice clears out?"

"I don't suppose," Seth said, closing the subject.

"How's the cannery pier?" Isaac asked.

"Well now, we've got some work to do there. One or two piles are loose. Don't know just how much yet."

"If it's bad enough, we might raise it up a foot or so. Wouldn't do any harm."

"We could get more rock underneath. It's weight we need."

And they were off on a familiar topic. Seth had spent most of his life working at the cannery as general maintenance man and had finally shifted to watchman with reluctance; but his real asset to the plant was still as planner and adviser in the endless task of rebuilding the pier. And for a hobby he worked on his own footbridge. It was the best game he knew—a sustained and personalized conflict. When they survived a bad winter gale he would say, "We got her licked that time"; and when the hurricane of 1954 smashed two sections of the pier and carried off the ice house as well he said, "She sure as hell got us this time." That with a wry grin too.

So the two of them spent an hour, sipping spiked coffee and talking timbers and bracing, hardly hearing the gale outside.

But there was the business part of the meeting too, and Isaac had a mind for business.

"Say," he said at last, "there's a small matter I don't want to forget."

"What's that?"

"Well, you might call it rent."

There was a pause. The ice grinding against the ledge out front was now as clear as if someone had opened the door. The house shuddered a bit as a gust slammed by.

"I don't believe you've asked for that before," Seth said at last, speaking slowly. "Seems like when I inquired about building out here, you just nodded. That was a time ago, of course."

"Twenty years this April first. Tomorrow."

"That's quite a memory for dates you have. And how much were you figuring I might owe you?"

"A dollar would do it, Seth."

"Dollar a year?"

"No, for the whole twenty." He finished his mug. "It's just a fluke of the law, Seth. Law says a man takes possession after twenty years unless he's renting." Seth didn't answer. "What I mean is, if a man lives in a place for twenty years. . . ."

Seth raised his hand for silence. "You're not telling me anything." He went to the wall where there was a calendar advertising "Granite Farms Pure Milk and Cream." He lifted the March sheet and pointed to the date of April 1. It was circled in red crayon.

"You sure as hell caught me this time," he said. "You've got more of the bastard in you than most folks realize." This with a wry smile. But then the smile vanished and he sat down again.

He squinted at Isaac, though at that distance he could see perfectly well. Then a hesitant smile came over his face again and he said, "Ike, is this your idea of an April Fool's trick? We're gettin' a bit advanced for that. . . ."

"No trick," Isaac said. He hadn't expected the resistance—just a dollar, after all. "This here's my land."

"Well for Lord's sake." It was as if Seth had only just then believed it. "You're serious."

"It's only a dollar I'm talking about."

"You can talk blue—you're getting no dollar from me."

"If it's the money, Seth, I could lend it to you."

"And hold possession for another twenty years? I don't fancy that."

"Then I'll deduct it from your pay."

"You'll deduct nothing. Not without my say-so."

"I've got the law, Seth, clear and straight. The land's mine."

"I've got the law too, when it comes to that. If I'm still sitting here at midnight, this here point is mine outright. I'm telling you, I'm not leaving. Not without being dragged. And you're not the man for dragging even the likes of me."

"For God's sake!" Isaac stood up, caught without words. Seth hadn't moved; he just looked up with a face flushed red. Then Isaac said in a rush, "You must be getting weak-headed. One dollar! You want me to go to court for one damn dollar?"

"You can go straight to hell for a dollar."

Isaac seized his coat and struggled into it, trembling with silent fury. He flung the door open. The wind slapped his face. "You're crazy out of your mind." he said and slammed the door behind him.

He stood there a moment, his rage sending tremors through his entire body. What could you do with a man like that? What the hell would it take to budge him?

Then he noticed that the wind had swung into the east a bit. Some of the ice slabs were being shifted, heaving murderously against the cannery pilings. From where he stood he could see that one corner of the loading platform had been weakened and now sagged. A wooden barrel of sawdust had already been dumped into the jumble of ice. No matter, He knew there'd be damage.

Then like the wind his mind shifted into a new quarter. There was hope after all.

Abruptly he turned and pounded on the door. "Seth," he called out. "Seth!" And as the door opened: "The pier. The cannery pier. We've got to get stuff out of there before the whole thing goes."

Seth peered by him, eyes squinting. "Something's smashed already," he said. "Wait up."

He disappeared but reappeared again in an incredibly short time, dressed in foul weather gear and boots. "Hurry up," he said, surging ahead along the footbridge, lumbering awkwardly in his boots. Isaac kept step right behind him as if driving him on.

They were half way across the bridge when Seth stopped dead. Isaac piled into him with a grunt of surprise. "Go on," he said roughly.

"I remembered. I just remembered." Seth was almost whining.

"You can't. . . ."

Isaac didn't want to hear him. He just pushed, grunting. "Go on," he kept saying, "Go on. Move. Go on." He pried at Seth's hand which was locked onto the railing.

They heaved against each other, almost evenly matched, senseless in their rage. Then Isaac raised his hand high and brought the edge of it down hard on Seth's wrist like a cleaver.

That did it. A squeal, a falling back, and a great rumbling like a line of boxcars being suddenly nudged, the sound resounding against his chest. Isaac felt a deep surge of power and then, catching sight of something larger out of the corner of his eye, turned just in time to see the whole front wall of his cannery pier buckle and slide toward the saw-tooth jumble of gray ice.

The freight-car rumble continued as the wall was wrenched free, slowly as in films, so that he could now see right into those rooms where he had spent his life. The floor heaved forward and objects started sliding toward the sea: a mop, two cleaning buckets, chairs, now the stainless-steel vat—the new one—and the freezer itself was beginning to rip from its fastenings. Upstairs the parts room dumped whole shelves of nuts, bolts, small hardware, and cases of empty cans on the ice like pepper; and there, incredibly, was his office and his old oak desk and swivel chair with green cushion sliding faster now with filing cabinets and then splintering down the back of a littered plank of ice. A file drawer split open like a flowerpot and the records of a lifetime flew like snow.

He neither moved nor spoke. It was outrageous. The brutality of it shocked him. It wasn't like other storms. There had been no contest. How was a man to fight back?

Then the bridge on which they were standing gave a sudden shudder.

"Seth!" he said, half in warning and half in fear. But Seth was clinging onto the railing and staring at the remains of the cannery with his mouth open. He was paralyzed. Isaac would have to act for them both.

He looked first toward the shore and then toward the island. The distance was equal. The planks under them lurched to a severe angle. He swung his arm around Seth and firmly guided him back out to his house.

By the time they were at the front door, the bridge behind Seth was on its side and going through slow convulsions.

"It too," Isaac muttered in disbelief. He held tighter to Seth as if they were still in immediate danger. Then he stumbled into the protection of the house and shut the door against all that brutality.

Inside, neither of them spoke. They sat there, panting, one on the bed and the other in a chair, staring at their own thoughts.

And why, Isaac asked himself, did I do a damn fool thing like that? If we were ashore now, I'd have broken his hold on this place easy as. . . .

Some great slab of gray ice in the twilight outside bellowed like a live thing—like Isaac himself when crossed. He shuddered and then tensed again as if reliving the crisis they had just passed through. Then he shook his head. Crazy thoughts, he muttered to himself, for a man my age.

"You're a hard, cold sonofabitch," Seth said, speaking slowly, staring at the floor. Isaac looked over at him sitting there on the edge of the bed. He was still in his foul weather gear, a crumpled pile of black rubber like something washed up after a storm . . . like bits and pieces from the wrecked cannery.

Alarm struck Isaac as unexpectedly as a slap of spray. Had he spent a lifetime on that miserable coast only to end up harsh as the sea itself?

"That's not so," he said sharply. "I brought you back out here, didn't I? The place will be yours."

"I don't want no gift."

"I don't take to giving."

"I've noticed."

"Fact is," Isaac said, thinking aloud now, "you wouldn't be worth a pile of rags if you were forced back into town."

"Nor would you." His voice was still no more than a mutter.

"Well, we'll get your bridge built again," Isaac said, lighting a kerosene lamp against the growing darkness. "Hell, I have to rebuild my own road every spring. No different. And the cannery—I can get that rebuilt too. There's money."

"But is there time?" Seth said.

They looked at each other squarely, but they chose not to answer the question. Seth stood up, finally, and shrugged off his foul weather gear. Then he lit the other lamp.

Later that night, after supper together, they played cards and drank hot whiskey. And when the sound of the ice occasionally broke through, Isaac sang ballads which he had known as a boy and which had lain dormant in him like seeds through the course of a long, hard winter.

Windy Fourth

It was Ike's idea that the family should enter the race again. And there was no objecting to that. It was, after all, his show. He had turned seventy that spring, and on July 4th he would celebrate his fiftieth anniversary. On the strength of that he had lured six of his eight children back to Maine—together with one son-in-law, three daughters-in-law, and a total of twelve grandchildren. The house was as full and noisy as it had been before the war—twenty years ago now. That was the way he wanted it. And it was just as important to have his "boys"—two of them into their forties by now—compete once again for the Farthington Neck handicap sailing trophy. He would have gone out himself if it weren't for his arthritis.

But from Jay's point of view, sitting there on the windward gunwale, the race was utterly absurd. It was not a question of discomfort. He was certainly used to that. There was even something invigorating about the slap of cold spray and the lurching of the boat. It was good to know that the years hadn't muted his old enthusiasms. The race itself, though—that was another matter. Even in good weather it would have been pointless—they all should have outgrown that sort of thing. And this was not good weather. It had been blowing hard out of the north at dawn and showed no signs of letting up by race time. Dark squall clouds slid by under the solid gray overcast, spitting rain. There was no sense in contending with all this just to revive the past for an old man.

Jay had nothing to do but act as ballast—a minor contribution for one so lean. His brother, Harry, was at the tiller, his red face bunched with sullen concentration. It would have been much better to have his bulk amidships, but having Harry at the helm was an old family tradition. They were twins—thoroughly unidentical—and Harry was senior by twenty minutes. Ike, the Old Man they called him, was a great one for recognizing seniority. Navy training—that's where they got it. The Old Man had served in the First World War and Harry, his first-born, had signed up in 1942. It gave the two of them something in common. But that was ancient history now. Jay shrugged, fending off old resentments.

Behind Harry's frowning face was the gray, white-flecked chaos of sea. All but three boats had quit the race. The McGuffrys' Rhodes 18 had capsized within four minutes of the start. The Zeltons' cutter had disqualified herself dramatically when the moldy mainsail went out with a whoosh, leaving nothing but absurd streamers. Shortly after that the Smythes and the Caldwells had veered off the course and headed back.

Jay grinned. There was something comic in seeing the show blown into a fiasco. He remembered for the first time in years the military review the Air Corps tried to put on when he was stationed in Biloxi, Mississippi. For a week they had scrubbed and painted that miserable base until it looked like something in a training film. But when the day came, so did the rains, and the drill field was covered with a foot of muddy water. The troops, bent low against the torrents, looked exactly like a vast collection of German P.O.W.s. The visiting generals were trapped on the little wooden reviewing stand like sodden roosters perched on a raft.

Remembering it made him laugh and he felt the salt crust on his cheek crack.

Harry saw the laugh and looked back at the other boats. Then he grinned too—though not at all for the same reason.

"Looks good," he shouted. "We'll win by default."

"So what?"

"I said—*we'll win by default.*"

"I heard you the first time."

"What?"

"Never mind."

"Never mind what? Speak up, Jay. I can't hear you over this damn wind."

Jay shrugged and looked forward. No point, he thought. Can't talk in weather like this. Can't get through to him. Hell, I never could. We don't know the same jokes. The race—there's a joke. But he won't laugh. Not Harry.

Jay kept his eyes on the sea. That was no joke. It was the simple, stark business of survival. No philosophy, no slogans, no reasoning; just staying alive. That's what made sailing alone the best kind; no little silver-plated trophy to win, no tricky set of handicap rules to argue about; just life. He remembered, smiling again, how he used to personify the sea, taunting it like an adolescent Odysseus when he was sure of himself, bargaining with it when he was in trouble. There was no time for that now—too many real hopes and fears to act on. Still, coming back here to this coast, these familiar ledges, these particular currents, was re-entering the church of his childhood.

And the sounds. That was a part of it too. It had been his cousin, Tina, who had taught him to listen. She had always had a good ear for that sort of thing. Whenever they went out together—which was often—they would catalogue everything they could hear: the hiss of water along the hull which was, on a day like this, angry. The rumble of the wet canvas edge, the roar of the wind which swept into the very pit of his ear; and, most ominous because it came only with gale velocities, the hum of vibrating shrouds. "Sounds like your father talking," she said once. But how could you describe all this to someone like Harry? Jay had given up years ago. For a decade they had exchanged nothing but fifteen-cent Christmas cards.

"Jay!" Harry was yelling at him again. "D'you want to quit? Is that it?"

"You're the skipper. Make up your own mind."

"How do *you* feel? I mean, maybe they've called off the race anyhow. We'd never hear the cannon from here." A surge of cold spray broke over them both. "Hell," Harry said, "you must be getting wet up there."

There it is! Brotherly compassion! He must be soaked through, but he won't admit it. He hasn't changed. Nothing's changed.

Jay caught a quick vision of what it would be like after the race: hot rum drinks around the fire, laughter, loud talk, and Harry, the heavy-hammed, hairy-armed cartoon of his father, telling how *Jay* was goddamn wet and cold and miserable and how *Jay* wanted to get back and how he, Harry, didn't really blame him, but how none of us were getting any younger, were we? That with a laugh. And the Old Man would laugh too. And then they would be off on what it was like serving convoy duty in the North Atlantic in January—the old-glory stories everyone in the family knew by heart.

"How about it?" Harry shouted.

"What?"

"I said, *how about it?*"

"How about what?"

"Turning back."

"Quitting?"

"Just say the word, Jay. It's O.K. with me."

That's all he needs. Just the word. And why not? When the party's over, I'll head back to California, back to all that. And Harry—he'll gather his brood and pile them into that ugly Buick and take them back to New York, back to his safe, solid old apartment. He'll slip back to his niche at Carlton, Brace and Whatsis, back to designing factories or whatever. The two of us, dear brothers, we'll go back to sending fifteen-cent Christmas cards—"Season's Greetings from Harry and Mildred Bates." Printed—that must cost him extra.

It was civilized that way. Neat. Mature. He had no objections. But the fact remained that in coming back he had been caught up in a private storm which was in no way civilized. It was an absurd, messy clutter of old feelings tossed in a jumble like flotsam from a forgotten wreck.

Only one fact was clear: he was damned if he was going to say a word and then be quoted as the one who sounded the retreat.

"It's your show," Jay said sharply. "Make up your own mind. Like in the Navy. Quick decision." He grinned to cover his anger, but Harry wasn't even looking. His little eyes were squinting at something just beyond the bow. Jay turned in time to see the black of solid water strike the deck, surge almost unbroken over the coaming, and pour into the cockpit.

Jay scrambled for the bucket, slipping, falling, recovering, now bracing himself with one foot propped against the almost vertical leeward seat. He bailed and cursed. They were bound to get wet, but piling right into one like that was just too much like Harry. He had no sense of timing. He sailed the way he used to play stud poker—with a kind of dogged respect for the book of instructions. "Determination," the Old Man called it.

"You still haven't answered," Harry said with that same determination. "Want to quit?"

"You're at the helm. It's your choice. Don't ask me. The Old Man wanted you at the helm. So make your own decisions."

"If *that's* it, here. You take it."

The offer came without warning. Jay started to protest. But already they were involved in the complex business of changing seats. The boat hesitated, luffing, sails rattling like a burp gun. There was no time for talk. As soon as Jay was set, he headed her off until she heeled again with a lurch and surged forward. It was good to feel the tiller in his hand.

"If you want to come about now," Harry said, "you'll have a nice, easy, down-wind run back to the mooring."

Neatly done, brother. Except I'm not coming about.

"What?" he said in mock horror. "And lose the race?"

"The race is over. Look."

As always Harry was right. The two boats from Henson's Cove were heading back, almost around the point now; and their younger brother, Joe, in the Herreshoff chartered for the occasion, had turned also, streaking for home on a broad reach. There was no one left on the bay now—not even a lobsterman. It looked more like a December sea—the way it had the last Christmas Jay had spent with the family almost twenty years ago. He remembered standing in the living room with his back to the warmth of the fire and family, looking down across the fields, the pines, the shale shore to that great gray expanse of churning cold sea, half drawn and half frightened, wondering idly whether he would endure as well in the war as that lean ledge called Peniel Island, two miles out there, had endured the winter storms.

Now, looking back over his shoulder, he could see part of the house, his father's pride, set high on the hill which swept back from the sea like a great leaden wave. They called it "The Farm" because that's what it had been for the whole of the nineteenth century. Isaac Bates bought it in 1919 for eight hundred dollars, a stiff price for him in those days even with his Navy bonus. Later, when there was more money, he added such luxuries as central heating and electric lights. But the only external change was the enormous plate glass window which he brazenly stuck in the front during the summer of 1927.

"It's too much window for me," Mrs. Bates always said whenever guests exclaimed about the view. "I'm not overly fond of the sea." She had her reasons. She had been born right there on Farthington Neck not five miles from where she ended up, and had a chance to see a lot of the Atlantic. She had seen her brother drown.

But her husband had been brought up inland in Massachusetts, cut off from the Atlantic by two generations. The sea had become a part of him or possibly, Jay sometimes thought, the reverse.

"We live on it," he reminded his children regularly. What he meant, of course, was *off* it as a result of his Bates Fish Products, Inc. It was his grandfather, William Bates, who was the last to really live *on* it.

But off or on, he needed it. In his younger days he used to sail whenever he could—often picking the worst weather. He went out with the lobstermen at least once a month—even in winter. He insisted they pay him cash for his labor. And now that he was trapped by arthritis he could not keep from staring out periodically, checking on the weather, the lobster catch, and the performance of sailboats. Nothing escaped him.

Jay had forgotten how little privacy there was on the bay. Once, after spending a sweltering and breathless day becalmed some five miles out, he was reprimanded severely for having picked his nose. And now looking back up to that house and that window he saw it as a displaced Cyclops, transplanted from the Aegean by some grotesque time-warp.

They were passing the buoy now which would have, had the race still been on, marked the turning point. It was a black can with "3" on the side and white gull droppings plastering the top like a birthday cake. It writhed in the heavy sea, straining at a 45 degree angle against the sweep of the tide.

Jay held his course. They were heading straight out to sea, just as he used to when he was a boy. He had no plan in mind. He knew only that he was not going to head back just yet. He was surer about that than he had been about anything in years.

"Leg bothering you?" Harry asked.

Jay looked up, confused. Then he realized he had been rubbing his bad knee, massaging it unconsciously. It was only a reflex. It hadn't troubled him for years.

"No."

"Looks like it's giving you trouble."

"It's O.K. now. Nothing wrong with it."

"Better not strain it."

The Old Man had used the same phrase that morning. "Let Harry take the helm," he had said. "That knee of yours—you don't want to strain it."

They don't seem likely to forget that, Jay thought. Not even if I do.

It had kept him on limited service in the Air Force, had kept him teaching mechanics in Mississippi. That's what Harry remembered. And Ike too. But the full story was more cluttered than that. In 1940, when Harry was finishing up at architectural school, Jay had quit college and was working for pacifists in the Midwest. He managed to gather 1,324 signatures—college boys who swore they would never fight. But by 1942, the outrage of fascism seemed greater than the sin of taking a life, so he signed up in the Army Air Force. "The Greatest Fighting Team in the World," they billed it. The decision wasn't easy. But having made it, he was prepared to test himself as a pilot or bombardier. That was when they discovered his trick knee.

He had proved nothing. His truest friends from the Ohio Peace Committee condemned him as a coward. His father wrote saying that to have a son on limited service was a "deep disappointment" and asked darkly why the knee had never bothered him before. Harry, that winter, sent the first of the fifteen-cent Christmas cards.

"What I mean," Harry said, scowling, "is that none of us are kids any more."

"So?"

"So why horse around out here? If you bang that knee, you may be in real trouble."

"Drop it. Forget it. I'm no cripple, you know." But he was getting too serious, so he forced a smile and added, "Sit back and enjoy it. We'll get back—eventually."

He hates uncertainty. Always has. Makes him squirm. Can't make a move without a compass course. But who can?

It was an old question for him, and it never failed to depress him. Those four years in Mississippi were directionless: he was neither a loyal pacifist nor a fighting soldier—nothing more, he wrote Tina, than a moral hermaphrodite. And Hiroshima didn't solve anything. It only got him out of Mississippi. He crammed his uniform into an ash can on East 40th Street, New York, and went to work for the United Nations Association. They put him on the speaker's bureau and billed him as an Air Corps Veteran. Corporal Bates, they called him. "They've got those stripes tattooed on my arm," he told Tina, and after a year he quit. He accused them of being politically bland—but that was only part of it.

It was Tina who got him into the Federalists. There was more life there. But raising funds for them was like fund-raising everywhere. By that time he and Tina had slid into marriage, and they worked together in a converted brownstone called Freedom House. The job lasted three years—and so did the marriage. No fights, no accusations; it was inexplicabale, like being becalmed just when you've come to depend on a steady southwest wind. That's when he headed for California. The scene changed, but the work was the same: fund-raising, chapter meetings, picketing, long and earnest talk into the black of night. "What on earth do you live on?" Harry wrote on one of those Christmas cards. "Faith," Jay answered on a postcard, but he didn't define the term. "Faith in sanity" was what he had in mind, but that would have confused Harry even more. He liked his slogans clear and familiar.

"Hates uncertainty," Jay said aloud, nodding to himself.

"*What?*"

"Nothing."

"Talking to yourself?"

"Reciting poetry."

"Reciting *what?*"

"Never mind. Forget it."

The wind came between them again. Jay looked down at his hand on the tiller. Here, at last, was a fragment of certainty. No dogma to argue—just a matter of holding the course and sailing into the heart of it for no reason than exercising his will.

The boat performed nicely. Even after all these years she felt familiar to him—an old friend unchanged. She was an eighteen-foot, Maine built, iron-keeled, gaff-rigged day sailor. She had been built in the early twenties, but the designer must have been a traditionalist because the *Whiskey Mary* looked like a ghost from the nineteenth century—indigenous as hell. For two decades she had been stored out of water, waiting. The Old Man had gone to some expense to have her refitted just for this race.

"Hey Jay!" Harry pointed to the Number 3 Can which was slipping well aft by now. "Come about!"

Jay squeezed the tiller and felt adrenalin course through him. He tried counting to ten, but by three a plan came to him. It sprang before him fully formed, nakedly idiotic, and seductive.

"Harry," he said, trying to shout in an affectionate tone, "why don't you bail?"

"What?"

"Bail. With the bucket. Water. . . ." He gestured. "Belongs outside."

Harry started to pick the bucket up and then dropped it—almost threw it.

"Look," he said, trying to read words in Jay's eyes, "what the hell are you doing?"

"Sailing."

"Where? Never mind why. Just where? How far out?"

"Around the island."

"Peniel? In this weather? We'll never make it." Spray caught him and must have reached clear down his neck because he suddenly hunched; Jay half expected him to shake furiously like a wet dog. "Will you turn this goddamned boat around?" Jay shook his head, adjusting the course just enough to let the boat slide off the brow of a roller. "Have you cracked up?"

"Cut the talking," Jay said, his voice sharp for the first time. "And start bailing. We'll swamp if you don't."

Harry started to come aft, his eyes—two dots in a red sea—were fixed on the tiller. Jay studied the next roller and instead of sliding down wind to ease the blow he held the tiller rigid. The *Whiskey Mary* slammed into the wave, shuddered as the water pounded on the deck, then heeled dangerously, throwing Harry in a jumble of arms and legs across the leeward seat.

After that Harry started bailing. But he couldn't help looking up periodically shouting "you're crazy" and "it's not so funny, you know" and "I tell you you're a sorry-sick-son-of-a-bitch" and "it's the last damn time I'm getting in this boat with *you*."

"Keep bailing," Jay said with a kind of tense good humor, and Harry kept bailing.

The rollers were larger now. Jay guessed that the tide had turned, was running against the swell, piling them up. And the wind had increased to the point where it began to break the crests, sending them off in gray streamers like the Zeltons' sail. Jay looked up at the aged canvas above him.

The *Whiskey Mary* rose on the back of a particularly majestic wave and hesitated with only an inch of freeboard before the descent. In the smoking distance Jay could see the bleak strip of island. The sea in that instant had caught the northwest corner—the far side—and a blast of spray spewed up over the black rock, towering like a geyser, then plunging downwind.

It was only a glimpse. But it was enough to make his stomach clench like a fist. He had forgotten how cold a ledge looked in rough weather. A tree or even a tuft of grass would have given it life; but there it was, wet rock in the middle of chaos. For the first time he truly regretted coming out.

But you're in it now, he told himself. Way in. Stick with it this time. No backing out. All the way, idiot.

Then he felt the boat plunge down the slick black slide and the island was lost. In fact all was lost: the horizon ahead and the land behind. The line in his hand eased and he realized that the waves were now high enough on either side to blanket the wind.

"Bail now," he said, no longer bothering to sound pleasant. "But jump back when the wind hits us. I need the weight to windward when we're on top."

Harry had given up answering. He caught two quick scoops and then as the boat heeled and the shrouds began that humming again he leapt for the windward seat, clinging to the gunwale like a great red-faced monkey.

Poor Harry—and the moment of compassion surprised him. Somehow Harry was no longer a part of this. He was just a passenger. The old resentments that had seethed in Jay during the past half hour now seemed muddled and distant—like their childish struggles for the biggest apple, the best baseball bat, the fullest bowl of porridge. Now there was only the simple, direct problem of circling the ledge without being drowned. And in answer to that minor voice within him asking "why?" he said "might as well—it's not going to get any worse." But he knew perfectly well that this was a lie.

"Easy, easy," he muttered aloud to the *Whiskey Mary* as she started to climb. "Up gently. That's it, up. This is a smooth one." And as they broke out into the screaming summit: "O.K., O.K., luff for a moment. Just wait. One more moment. Hush now, damn it. O.K. *now!*" And they would shoot down again, sail filled, rushing over black water streaked with the white of shattered foam, down into the black of the trough. Then it would start again.

At one crest he looked back over the wilderness to the mainland. It was solid and gray, a substantial mass of rock topped with gunmetal trees. He didn't have time to pick out The Farm except in his mind's eye. His brothers, Joe and Penn, would be peeling off wet clothes, layer after layer, hanging them on chairs around the living room fire, taking sips of scalding rum, laughing with the Old Man, with their sister Cory, about a mooring missed, an almost-swamp, a wave smack in the face. Mother would smile—a strong sun showing through overcast. No rum for Mother, but strong country hands hanging parkas, pants, arranging wet sneakers, moving restlessly, happy to have something to do in that farm which was no longer farming, no longer demanding anything but wattage and solvency. And above it all like the hum of shrouds was the cavernous voice of the Old Man, the voice that had drawn them all back through a series of phone calls, the voice which now, surely, rumbling past wide-lensed field glasses, must be saying, "What's he doing? Around Peniel just for the hell of it? In this weather? What in God's name's got into him?"

And Jay, hearing the words—even the tone of them—at long distance without benefit of wire, smiled and fixed his attention on the waves with a kind of grim affection described by the Jewish prophets as love.

They were abreast of Peniel now and the sound of the waves blasting at rock came through to them. In a single vision Jay could see them forced down on that rock, pounded on it, smashed.

He shifted course and began to pass the far side. Frequently the entire outline of the island was lost in burning foam and an instant later the thunder would reach them. Jay passed as close as he dared, circling the black rock like a moth twisting around a lamp. Harry had stopped bailing, clung to the cowling and stared at the rock, his face twisted.

They were halfway around now and were traveling across the wind on a broad reach. They were taking on less water over the bow, but it was increasingly difficult to keep the rolling boat from dipping its soaked sail in the sea. It would take the sea only one firm grasp to suck them over. And it took no imagination at all to visualize them in the water, the sail flat on the sea, a jumble of lines, seats, buckets, and the rush toward the rock.

"Easy," he said to the boat to soothe her, calm her, keep her from panic. "Easy does it. No mistakes now."

He had just said it when he realized that he had already made a mistake. A bad one. Stupid! Incredibly stupid. Had he come around the island the other way he could have safely come about and headed back. But this way, the way he had come, he would have to jibe.

One solution, the sloppy solution, the safe solution, would be to make a complete circle to avoid the danger of a jibe. But somehow that would spoil it. No logic, of course. But if he was going to be an ass he might as well be a perfect ass.

"Going to jibe," he yelled at his brother. But the words came out muffled. "Harry. . . ."

Harry turned and shook his head. He had heard and was objecting. His face had turned gray like the sea.

Jay wanted to say something kindly, something brotherly, but he was too busy. He cleared the sheet, unwrapping it from around his foot. Then he coiled the free section, loosely, dropping it near him as his father had taught him.

They had turned so the rollers swept in on them from the stern, but on enough of an angle so that each one lifted the boat and swept it closer to the rock. It was time to jibe.

Quickly he hauled in on the sheet until the sail was tight, flat, expectant. Then he slammed the tiller past him until it struck the gunwale. For one second the line went slack in his hand: then there was a "woosh!" as the sail shot across perfectly, the line slipped neatly through his hand, burning slightly. But no: the line snagged on a cleat, it drew tight, snapped. The sail continued on out until the boom was perpendicular to the boat and there, unattached, it flapped wildly like a wounded gull. The frayed end of rope dangled over the water, just beyond reach. The *Whiskey Mary* wallowed drunkenly, rolled wildly taking on green water, swung broadside to the swell and, passive now, surged toward where the surf was pounding.

"Stay there," Jay shouted, but there was no need. Harry was rigid, his big hands frozen to the shroud.

Fumbling, Jay released the jib. It too joined the bedlam of thundering canvas. Then he threw himself forward to the point where the boom met the mast. Bracing his foot against the cowling, he pulled the boom in toward the center of the boat. But he was straining against the full force of the wind. A curling wave caught them on the windward side and sent a new torrent of water into the boat. He kept his eyes on the varnished spar in his hands.

Then, unexpectedly, they descended into a particularly deep trough. The boom swung toward him, as obliging as if they were becalmed. He jumped aft, stumbling over the bucket, and with a leap snagged the end of the boom with a length of line. As they came up out of the trough the wind slammed against them, a great hand against the flat of the sail. The water poured in. Then she responded, surging forward.

And at once the crisis was over. Incredibly. The rock slipped behing them and grew smaller; each wave, now that they were sailing down wind, lifted them gently and swung them forward. The wind, with them now, no longer cut and no longer hummed in the shrouds.

Jay stood, holding the line in one hand and the tiller between his legs.

"Well," he said with a grin, "I guess we'll head back now."

Harry did not answer. He was on his knees bailing the water which slopped back and forth in the cockpit the way it used to in the tub when they bathed together.

"Jay," he said after a while, "you must be clear out of your mind."

But there was no anger left in his voice. It was not even the voice of an older brother.

"Crazy stunt," Jay said smiling. "I know. But we made it."

"No thanks to me. I'll bet you had the Old Man sweating too."

"I imagine so."

Jay looked up at that frowning coastline until he spotted the glint of the plate glass window. Then he set his course by it.

The Tide and Isaac Bates

He'd wrecked her. No doubt about that. He'd been careless and his luck had run out, finally, and what was a man to do then?

He was standing high on the bluff they had just climbed. Below him his *Diana* lay broadside to the wind and to the fist of the sea. Each breaker drove her hard against the black raw edge of the ledge. Her cockpit was flooded, her decks awash. There was no saving her now. It was enough to make an old man sick.

"Rest here," he said to Cory, his daughter. "Catch your breath."

He started to reach out, to reassure her. But, hell, she was all of twenty-five and still a tomboy—she could take whatever came along. Besides, how can you offer an encouraging hand to someone done up in lobstermen's rubber pants and hooded jacket? Almost his height, she could have been some fisherman's adolescent boy, tall, lean, and undernourished. Her thin lips were tight and a little blue with cold, but her expression was blank. She wasn't complaining. Hell, she could shrug off anything.

A wave of exhaustion swept over him without warning and he sat down in the coarse brown grass, his muscles trembling. Carefully he reached under his torn yellow slicker, under his leather jacket, down to the wool shirt where he kept his cigarettes and matches. They were in a plastic case. He took out one cigarette and the box of wooden matches and tried to strike a light, his hands cupped against the November wind. The head of the first match came off like putty.

The second merely smeared the striking edge of the box. It hardly seemed fair. Silent, drained of profanity, he put the case back into his inner pocket and chewed on the end of the cigarette.

All this time his eyes never left his boat. Four, five, six breakers had come and washed back. Turning his head, he spat tobacco juice downwind. Then a leviathan wave lifted his *Diana* up on her side, cracked her on the solid face of the ledge, sucked back and let the hull jounce after it. This time the shock shattered everything above deck, canopy, cabin and all scattering into bits of flotsam, the glass of the windshield exploding noiselessly into an instant of glittering spray. Isaac Bates heard himself utter a startled "Aaa!"

And then, embarrassed, he said to Cory, "Well, it's just a matter of time now."

He tried to make it sound offhand. The two of them never talked much about their inner feelings. They got along best just sharing chores—repairs around the house, chopping wood, or sometimes going over the books down at the cannery. The rest of the time she helped her mother. If anything bothered her, she didn't feel obliged to tell him, and in return he didn't burden her with his own worries. Of the eight children, she was the only one who would stay home, and he wasn't about to drive her away.

So there were times—like on early-morning crow hunts or off fishing somewhere—when her eyes would fill with tears for no reason and he wouldn't ask why. And right now he had cried out and she had said nothing.

Because it *was* nothing, really. The *Diana* wasn't his livelihood, nothing fundamental had been shattered, there was insurance and he wasn't poor anyway; they had not been injured, and they were lucky to have ended up on the mainland rather than on some tide-scoured ledge. Cory knew all that. She had a level head, she did.

Again the dark November water slithered back, and this time he saw that her hull had been stove in. There was no longer any hope of salvage. Isaac squeezed his eyes shut, wincing from the sting of salt. He would not look at her in that November way. He would see her as she had been twenty-two years ago, newly built and still unpainted,

red oak planking pink as a baby's rump, the admiration even of
strangers.

Maine craftsmen had built her, some of them using the hand tools
their fathers had given them. The oak itself came from Isaac's own
woodland, a section so rough that only oxen could get the logs out to
the truck on the highway.

"What's a man like you messin' around with a *lobster* boat for?"
That's what Elias Skolfield had asked when the *Diana* first took
shape on his ways. He wasn't being critical; he wasn't even asking a
question. He was simply approving the design, nodding because she
was to be the solid, high and dry design of the Maine coast lobster
boat. He was also noting the fact that Isaac Bates was no simple
fisherman, that the slogan "You Can't Beat Bates for Frozen
Fishcakes" had done more than pay off the mortgage. A man in
Isaac's position—at his crest then at only thirty-six—might easily
have invested in one of those factory-built speedsters. But he hadn't.

"Well, it's got honest lines," Isaac said, his trumpet muted as it
had been for the birth of all eight children.

"*Proud* lines," Skolfield said. There was just a bit more sheer to
her than the average lobsterman, but only a builder would have noticed it. "And power enough for three boats."

"Good to be on the safe side," he said, but he was thinking about
the feel of the throttle and the lurch forward at his command.

As they talked there in the yard, the shifting May breezes brought
to Isaac odors of cedar planking, mahogany shavings, tar and pine
pitch. The sun was warm in his face and anticipation radiated in him
like a good rum.

"Let's go," someone was saying.

He watched a shipbuilder on *Diana*'s deck take wood plugs from a
keg and hammer them into drilled holes, setting each with the first
blow and driving it home with two more. With his left hand he
caresssed the surface before setting the next, checking the level of
each plug, a regular motion, rhythmical. . . .

"Let's go now."

Rhythmical as waves, breakers pounding. . . .

"Come on now," Cory was saying. "We'd better get moving."

The November gale suddenly tore at his face again. His cheeks felt raw. He looked down at the ledge below them and then quickly up at Cory. She had taken off her bulky foul weather pants and stood there in wet, clinging Levi's. The hood of her jacket was thrown back now. Her hair, sand-colored and stringy, was soaked. He felt a rush of concern for her. She was a strong girl, but still. . . .

Pulling his sleeve up, he tried to read his watch. The crystal was clouded with droplets on the inside.

"Your watch working?" he asked her.

She reached up under her jacket and pulled out her wrist watch from some dry pocket. She looked at it and put it to her ear.

"It's working," she said.

"What time is it?"

"Five fifteen."

"Well, it's turned now. It's on the ebb. Might as well go."

He had planned to wait until the tide had passed its peak at five. There had been a slim chance that some boat might have passed and with the tide still on the flood they might have tried to get her off. The odds of that were hard against him, of course. The tourists were all gone by Labor Day and half the lobstermen quit for the winter by the first of November. What few remained wouldn't tour the traps on an afternoon like this. Still, a man had to be an optimist if he was going to get a thing out of life.

Like coming through the gut in the first place. He and Cory had navigated that channel between Black Island and the mainland a number of times. It was risky, of course, but there was always enough water so long as they were twenty minutes before or after the peak of the tide—always until today. Still, for all this, he didn't regret the other times. Summer folks used to shake their heads, seeing them run through a channel that was naked ledge at half-tide. A man had to take chances just for the sake of living.

Like having women friends. It was no mean trick for a married man in a small town like that to have his pleasures on the side. His old Mercury sedan was familiar all over that part of Maine. Even school children knew that he was the one that owned the cannery. And the risk of hurting his wife was a real one since his love for her was honest and full. Ella was a good woman. But any man worth his salt had to run risks just to keep himself alive.

"There was still a chance to save her," he said, "until her side was stove in . . . if only someone had come along before the tide changed."

"It won't change for another hour," she said flatly. "It won't be high until 6:00."

He looked up at her sharply, squinting. It wasn't like her to contradict. "Not that it makes any difference now," she added.

"It was high at five," he said. "Just fifteen minutes ago."

That settled, he heaved himself up and with a grunt set the duffle bag on his shoulder. It held all they were able to salvage from the *Diana*—her personal effects, so to speak.

"Got to get to the highway before dark," he said. Then he set off with his back to the sea, assuming that Cory would follow close behind.

The grass bluff gave way to a tangle of spruce and hemlock with clumps of briar between which waved like whips in the wind. As they moved inland, the sound of the surf died behind them, but always there was the moan from the treetops. It was growing dark much more suddenly than he had expected. He wanted to stop and try looking at his watch again—perhaps the condensation had cleared. It was an uneasy feeling to have the crystal clouded like that. He hated having to depend on Cory's. Still, what time *was* it? And when was sunset?

They walked for what must have been an hour—or was it only half that long?—all the time expecting to come out on the highway. Somehow it retreated darkly before them. His luck was still bad.

Suddenly he heard his wife Ella cry out from her hospital bed. He stopped dead. Time hung motionless in the twilight.

"An owl," Cory said flatly. "Did you hear it?"

So they continued without a word. An owl. Yes. Of course. He had taught her to identify the cry of birds and she had been a good student. So much for that.

But the picture of Ella lingered there in the gloom. Poor Ella in a strange city in the miserable hospital bed, alone and wondering what would become of her next month. She was strong—she was strength itself—but she'd never had to face anything like this.

"First trip to a hospital in eighteen years," she had said with that taut smile of hers. That was only three days ago. Eighteen years previous she had given birth to the last of their eight children. It was, he remembered, quickly done, neat and on time. Just like her. And in those days the nurses and friends always commented on how strong she was, how healthy. But this time the swelling in her uterus was not a new life. It was a lump which at best was bad. The doctors in Portland had consulted, tested, and talked more. So Isaac made some long distance calls, told Cory to pack, and drove the three of them down to Phillips House, the expensive wing of the Massachusetts General Hospital in Boston.

The first thing he did there was to tell the doctor in charge that in any event he was to "talk straight." Then, sitting awkwardly on the edge of the easy chair in Ella's private room, he made plans for the family:

"This may take time," he told them. "And I don't intend to do much commuting. So as soon as we get the place closed up and the *Diana* over to the yard for the winter, Cory and me will find a hotel room nearby."

"Don't go to all that trouble," Ella said. "I'll be all right."

"No trouble. Never did think much of a Maine winter anyway," he said, echoing his own annual refrain.

"Been suffering in silence?" she said with a hint of a smile.

A wave of affection caught him off balance.

"Only thing that makes me suffer," he said, "is having you in this goddamned nunnery instead of where you should be."

"Never you mind about that," she said. Then she began with a long list of things which would have to be done at the house: kitchen cleaned, refrigerator emptied, linen packed away.

"I sure hate leaving all this to you two," she said, shaking her head. "But I guess I've got no choice."

That struck him hard. She was right, he supposed. But it was a terrible thing to hear someone utter the words "no choice." Worse than dying. Perhaps the same.

And now, in this miserable, darkening forest, did he have any choice? He was heading for the highway with his head down, driving one foot before the other, mindless.

When they finally broke through onto the tar road they almost fell, stumbling giddily. The rhythm of effort had been interrupted. Legs tingling, they turned this way and that in the middle of the road, surprised and without plan. What had been a gray, fast-moving overcast was now a dark, blood-tinted haze. Looking up he saw three gulls flying hard and into the wind. It was a bad sign—only during the worst of gales did they risk crossing straight through the center rather than riding it out.

"Rest yourself," he said. "Someone's bound to come by."

They waited, sitting silently in the winter-killed grass next to the road, leaning against the duffle. He tried to take a look at his watch again, but even when he turned it so as to catch the last dull glow from the sky, he could not see the hands.

After a time—more or less—a pickup truck came by and stopped without Isaac having to make a gesture. He slung the duffle in back and got in the cab. Cory climbed in after him.

"Mr. Bates?" the driver asked. His voice was adolescent. He sounded like one of the Skolfield grandsons, but Isaac could never tell them apart.

"Right," Isaac said. "You're one of the Skolfields?"

"Pete."

They drove in silence. As they passed a cluster of three houses by the general store, Isaac noticed a kerosene lamp in the window of one. The electric line was down again. But there was no need to comment.

Finally the boy gave in to his curiosity. "Been hunting?" he asked.

"Lost my boat," Isaac said. "Had to beach her."

That wasn't really honest, of course. He had driven her hard on the ledge. An incredible miscalculation. Baffling. No, he hadn't

beached her; he'd wrecked her. But how could you say that aloud?
"It's a bad night," the boy said.

When they came to Isaac's mailbox the boy turned in without a word. It was a five-minute drive in over that rutted dirt road and another five out, but the boy was offering his time as condolences.

When they came out on the hillside where Isaac's house and barn were, they were hit with the gale again. The truck shuddered with a gust before they drew into the lee of the house itself.

"Can we get her off at dawn?" the boy asked as they got out. "Tide's high again at six-thirty."

"*Five*-thirty," Isaac said sharply. "Besides, it's too late. She's broke up."

A wave of despair broke over him. He opened his mouth to say thanks, but he couldn't utter a word to the boy. What did *he* know about such things?

"You're lucky to be alive," the boy said.

"You think so?"

But Isaac's answer never reached the boy; it was lost in the wind and in the decades that lay between them. The headlights swung sharply and soon were only a winking flicker through the forest on the other side of the pasture, streaking back to town, leaving the night blacker than ever.

They entered the kitchen like two blind strangers. It hardly seemed possible: for more than twenty years the house had been filled with children—eight of them in the peak years. They had gone, one by one. Scattered. And was there, finally, only this blackness? Was that all?

The power must have been off for hours, for without the oil furnace going the place had picked up the dank, tomb-like chill of a house long deserted. Isaac flipped the light switch from habit and the blackness became more intense. He shivered, groping for matches.

When in doubt, Isaac gave orders. "Find a flashlight," he said to Cory. "And get the kitchen matches." It didn't pay to speak softly if you wanted action. "We need about four lamps going. Start with the

ones in the pantry." They hadn't had electricity in the place until
1935 and a part of him had always resented all that too-easy glare.
"Then get some spills for the range."

He groped about for a flashlight, but before he could locate one
there was a flicker of orange behind him. She was lighting the lamp.
The room appeared and the storm outside was forced back hissing.

"Now some kindling," he said. She lit a second lamp for her own
use and then tossed to him the matches and a fresh pack of
cigarettes. When she was safely out in the woodshed, he began to
study the tide chart which was hanging on the wall. His hands ripped
carelessly at the cigarette package as he squinted to make out the
blur of fine print. "November . . . November . . . November 10, High
. . . ." He lit a cigarette and inhaled deeply. "November . . . 10 . . .
High *5:05*."

"Ha!" He whooped and called to Cory.

But the black wave which had sucked back for an instant
thundered down on him once again: November 10th they had driven
Ella to Boston. And the 11th they were still there. This was the *12th*.
He put his hands to his temples. Gears had slipped.

"Was that you?" Cory asked. She was standing there at the door
with a coal hod half-filled with the spills—wood chips and bark.

"Me? No," he muttered, taking the hod from her. "Just the
wind." He started laying the fire.

She didn't question it. He could hear her behind him, bustling
about like a young Ella, lighting lamps, stuffing wads of paper in the
windows that rattled, mopping the front hall where the rain had
driven under the door, filling jugs of water from the last remaining
trickle from the faucet. When his fire was roaring with pine slabs he
converted to oak and she put the kettle on the hottest section of the
stove.

"You'll be needing a hot whiskey, I suppose,"; she said in an offhand, affectionate way. The echo of Ella was startling.

"We both will tonight."

"Now don't get me all giddy," she said, setting the kitchen table
for two with quick motions. "I've a lot to do tonight."

He didn't press it, seeing her set out two white mugs. That was something has wife would never have done—not once over the course of decades. And there had been times—like this one—when it would have been good to have shared a drink.

She brought him the bottle of King's Whiskey and he measured by eye a double shot for them both, the slosh in each mug as quick and accurate as a bartender's. Then she filled each with steaming water from the kettle.

"Sugar and lemon for yours," he said. "Nothing for mine."

He watched her as she went to the pantry and sliced lemons. It seemed senseless to him to have pants cut like that. All the young folks were wearing them. He sniffed the steam from his drink and felt sweat come to his forehead.

"You should get out of those wet things," he said abruptly.

"They're drying out."

"Women shouldn't wear pants anyhow."

"First I've heard you complain," she said lightly. She was holding her mug in both hands, warming them, and taking quick sips.

"Just change them."

The smile went from her face. He thought he saw a flicker of fear there and cursed himself for speaking roughly to her. Still, why not? She hadn't been raised to be just another fair-weather girl. Not like the other two—fooling around with men too old for them and stumbling into marriage and moving away. No, Cory had her feet squarely on the ground.

And as if to prove it she obeyed him by heading up the stairs to her room. She was back down only half a mug later with sweater and skirt over her arm.

"It's winter up there," she said. "Turn around so I can change without freezing."

He faced the stove, his mug in hand, and listened as her wet Levi's hit the floor with a splot and her dressing filled the room with a charged silence. The heat from the range prickled his face.

"Stove heat makes sense," he said, speaking only to hear his own voice. "You know just where it comes from. Keeps people together.

As soon as you put in a furnace, the family scatters all over the house, each to his own damn room. Good feeling to have the heat at your face and cold at your back."

"So who put the furnace in?" she asked, hanging her wet clothes up on the pegs behind the range.

"Ella did," he said. It was meant as a kind of easy joke, but strangely the name of Ella cast a pall on the place. Cory paused, hand on peg, and took in a deep breath. Isaac took a scalding slug of his drink. He wished he hadn't brought her name into that kitchen. She was gone. He and Cory had the place to themselves.

"Will she live?" Cory asked very quietly.

"Live?" It was a rotten question to ask about a dying woman. "Of course she'll live. Good God, don't you know that *all* wives outlive their men? What's the matter with you, d'you want to wish her right into her grave?"

She was looking at him now, her mouth open, her eyes squinting, and face pale.

"Oh, come on, now," he said, jovial again, "don't take everything so serious."

"Sorry."

"Nothing to be *sorry* about. You sound like your Uncle Will." She grinned. His older brother, William, was a perpetual victim. The very mention of his name brought smiles in Isaac's home. "Like when he was trying to teach your cousin Tina how to drive. . . ."

"And was standing in the garage?"

"So as to direct her in backing out. . . ."

"But she wasn't in reverse?"

"In first. That's right." They were both laughing now. "So Uncle Will gets pinned to the wall. . . ."

"Between the studs?"

"That's all that saved him. And she gets flustered and shouts at him. . . ."

" 'Why do you have to stand right in front of me?' "

"And he says," Isaac could hardly finish. " '*Sorry.*' "

Isaac wiped the tears from his eyes and poured more whiskey in each mug. It was the first time he had told the story without Ella shaking her head and saying "Poor Will." Cory added the hot water to his drink from the kettle. She hesitated over her own mug, then shrugged and added the water.

"You won't tell on me?" she said with a grin.

"I wouldn't tell on my Cory," he said.

"You may just have to do without supper."

"There's more in this world than a goddamned series of home-cooked suppers."

"Let's drink to that," she said. They clinked mugs. "No more meals, no more brooms."

" ' . . . No more teacher's dirty looks,' " he chanted.

"Doesn't rhyme."

"Say, did I ever tell you about your Uncle Will and the mop salesman?"

"Never," she said. He knew she was lying, but neither of them cared. He loved the telling and she loved the listening so he started right in. The pieces of the story fitted together, link by link, building. Then, finally, at precisely the right moment they exploded into laughter.

After a lull he said, "You know, we're goddamned lucky to be alive."

"Sure are," she said. "You've got a genius for picking the right ledge to land on."

He snorted a laugh right in the middle of a gulp. Whiskey sprayed the air. They broke into laughter again. The sound sent him back years to a rooming house in town and some Latvian woman named . . . what *was* her name? But by heaven she could laugh. From the gut. Free and open. God she loved life. And everyone else. Danced until you were out of your pants and then brought you down with a whoop.

"No one really loves a cook," he said to Cory, sloshing a careless round into their mugs. "A man who hauls himself off a black ledge doesn't cry out for a meal. No sir!"

"And what *does* he cry for?" She was heading for the kettle.

"Celebration. Thanksgiving."

"So you shall have it," she said, kettle in hand. "Today is a holiday."

"Celebration for being alive."

"We'll have one every day. This place *needs* a celebration every day. Forever."

She was pouring the water with a flourish, kettle a foot above the mugs. It splashed over the table, steaming. Some ran from the table onto his pants and he jumped up, laughing.

"God but you're sloppy," he said, delighted with her. The room turned on its mooring; the deck rose and fell under him. The kettle went somewhere and she was laughing, her head back, and he was holding her, dancing about the room singing 'O Sole Mio!" and feeling her close against him and laughing and his hand drove itself down beneath the fabric of her skirt onto the round of a buttock firm as youth itself and the other hand wrenched at the cloth, ripping it.

Her fingers were suddenly at his face, ripping like winter spray. He threw her back from him and with a crack of timbers she went down hard.

He staggered back, sober. She was lying there on the floor, broadside to the black cookstove, rocking. Her hands were over her face; she began sobbing like the winds, lost.

Later that night, the electric lights glared back on. That was when she stood again, solemn, dry-eyed, white, and unreal. Ghostlike.

"We'd better eat something," she said.

She heated some tasteless spaghetti. Silently they ate, knowing that it would be the first of many like that—just the two of them there like figures in a waiting room, afraid to touch each other even with words.

Grubbing for Roots

Erik woke, sat up abruptly. The iron springs squealed under the weight of his bulk. From downstairs Sal's voice—the sound that had jolted him awake—continued. . . .

"I said stop it now before . . . . Oh *no!*" Then, her voice weary, "God, your father will be furious. Honestly, Michael, you must be psychotic."

Well, it was done. No use worrying—particularly on his day off. So Michael had gouged the kitchen table with his wood-block carving or broken a window or. . . . No, it was something father-owned. Erik frowned, concentrating. Had he left his axe out? The chain saw? The possibilities were limitless. Michael, seven, was the dreamer, the reader. Only last Christmas he had been left to watch a batch of inkberry brew on the cookstove—a dye they used for decorations—and with his head in a book he had let it boil right down to a stinking scum. The house had smelled for a week.

With Michael it was always daydreaming carelessness. But with Timmy, two years younger, it was cheerful rebellion. Once he had dismantled the family typewriter in less than an hour.

On such occasions Erik bellowed, spanked, roared protests, had everyone in tears. But he held no grudges. For the first time in his life he owned land, plenty of it, and that gave them room for error. No upstairs tenants to complain about the noise. Not even neighbors. This was a place where he and his family could work out their problems directly. For all the destruction that went on, their life there was far less damaging than the tight-lipped, dour, and oppressive world he had endured as a boy back in St. Louis.

He threw off the covers and shivered. It was April and still raw. Spring comes slowly in upstate Maine, and this was still the mud season. He swung his feet onto the floor, each one striking the cold boards like a slab of beef. The windows rattled.

From where he sat he could look down on the shingled woodshed roof still white with frost but now beginning to steam from the warmth of the sun. Beyond was the barn, swaybacked and wavesided in the swirls of old window-glass. He thought of all the calculations that had once gone into that barn, careful measurements to the inch, ridgepole made to match the horizon of the sea with a spirit level, uprights aimed directly at the center of the earth with a plumb bob; all that planning, yet it looked far better to him through this old glass, no two lines parallel or even straight.

His neighbors, country bred, probably wouldn't see it that way. But Erik's childhood had been straight-edged, straight-backed, with plumb lines drawn right to the heart of the lower middle class. He wanted no more of that. Neither he nor Sal wanted any more of that.

"He won't take you with him," Timmy was chanting to his older brother. "He won't take you. He won't take you."

"He will too."

"Won't!"

"Hush up, both of you. Try being quiet. Just try."

"We'll be quiet as . . . mice," Michael said, pleased with the simile.

"No," Timmy said. "Quiet as ghosts."

"There aren't any ghosts."

"There are."

"*Silence!*" And she was granted it.

But of course there were ghosts. For Erik that was a good part of the farm. The Skolfields, for example—distant relatives of Sal's. Generations of them had bred cattle in the barn where Erik now kept his Jeep and four Nubian goats. Skolfields had bred Skolfields on the creaking, squealing bed he slept in. And when they died, they didn't go far. Down behind the barn, just barely within view of that upstairs bedroom, was the family cemetery, stones half-hidden in the untended grass. There were generations lying there, though he hadn't had time yet to sort them all out.

There had come a time when the cities began to seduce the survivors—Sal's branch moving south to Kittery. It was the same pull which had drawn Erik's family off the Missouri farm into St. Louis and the servitude of a retail business. The Maine farm went on the market and was eventually bought by a wealthy out-of-stater who was generally regarded as crazy. His goal in life was to save the Arctic musk ox from extinction. Maine, apparently, had the right combination of fodder and isolation. They didn't mind the cold and they needed space for grazing. Some he brought down from the Aleutian Islands at great cost; others he wheedled from zoos where they were prone to be sickly and irascible. The neighbors, tolerant yet highly conservative in their husbandry, predicted disaster.

Erik had heard from them grim tales of bulls that gored their young and cows gone sterile. A pack of troubles, they said. But for all this the herd did grow. There was a time when those hillside pastures were dotted with the shaggy and foreign-looking beasts. The juniper bushes through which they wandered were adorned with long wisps of fur finer than cashmere.

So the experiment was a success. But no one cared, possibly because there was no real money in it. The story was that he needed more land and moved further north—to New Brunswick or perhaps Newfoundland.

As soon as the farm was on the market a second time, a distant cousin wrote Sal's aunt, wondering if someone in that great extended family would by the place back. They had a high regard for continuity.

The decision to move to Maine was too big for them to have made with logic and planning. Chance put the pieces together. As lovers they had shared an aching dislike for the college they were both attending and for the city in which it was located. Even in winter they would seek out deserted beaches along the Rhode Island coast and walk for miles, their silent pleasure a kind of communication. For him, college was an entrapment. He had been lured there by parents who saw it as financial security; and when they told him how much they had sacrificed to keep him there, it was like locking the gate of a cage. How could he leave?

He could never tell them how he spent his hours in class imagining himself smashing every window in the room with his fist. Or that he had dreams of knocking down walls. The only person he could confess that to was Sal.

They both wanted to break out, but the escape route was unclear. Where would they go? Both of them had grandparents who had farmed, but everyone knew that you couldn't do that anymore—not without making a business out of it. And neither Erik nor Sal was drawn to communes. So they remained in captivity and graduated with honors.

Freed, they stepped right into another trap. They tried teaching in an urban school. It was the Right Thing to be doing, but horrible. Then, in a single week, their apartment was robbed, they were served with an eviction notice from the Highway Department, and they received the news about the farm in Maine. Never mind that the place was without telephone, electricity, and running water; even without seeing it they had made the decision.

Voices drifted up again. They were arguing about boots. That meant breakfast was over and he had wasted more time than he should even for a Sunday. He planned to put in four hours at the boat yard that day, extra work to make up for the long, jobless winter.

"But there's no snow," Michael was saying.

"There's mud," she said. "The road is a veritable quagmire."

"What's 'veritable?' " That from Timmy.

"To you, kiddo, 'irresistable.' Now get those boots on."

"But they're so heavy," Michael said.

"Builds leg muscles."

"And make us strong?" As the youngest, Timmy was on a

strength kick.

'Incredibly strong.''

"As strong as Daddy?"

"Almost."

"When I'm grown up. . . ."

"Get that damn boot on."

"When I'm grown up. . . ."

"The boot."

"But when I'm grown up will I be as big as Daddy?"

"At least. Hold still now, I'll do it."

"And I'll have a car. And be tall."

"Sure you will."

"And have a big wee-wee like. . . ."

"Right. Now stamp on that boot."

"A giant has a wee-wee as big as my arm."

"There aren't any giants. Now the other boot."

"But if there were?"

"As big as your arm. At least."

"Wow! Hey Michael, did you hear that? Mom says. . . ."

"Knock it off, kids. Get those damn boots zipped." Her voice was brusque. "O.K. out, both of you." The door slammed and there was silence. Erik grinned and began dressing.

When Erik came down the stairs, the house shook. He liked the sensation. When the boys were there, he would thunder out "Fee, Fi, Fo, Fum," one syllable for each step. But this time there was only Sal and he couldn't be sure what her mood would be. Three months pregnant, she was having a hard time with mornings.

And then too, there was the matter of his working weekends and evenings at the boat yard. She could see the sense of it—for the length of a bitter winter he had not worked more than two days a week. It was half a day here helping to plaster the church basement and a day there shoveling crap out of a four-story chicken barn. What few lobstermen went out didn't need help and the boat yard lay silent and unheated. Now at last he was offered work seven days a week if he could stand it, and he could damn well stand it. It would be two months before all the lobster boats and the few pleasurecraft were scraped, painted, and hauled out of that sagging, leaking old boathouse and launched. And for the rest of the summer he would be kept busy as hired hand on lobster boats and tending his goats and his garden.

Right now he had to earn some cash and she knew it. But she was also feeling dependent. He wasn't used to that.

As he came into the kitchen she was at the soapstone sink, scraping the breakfast dishes into the triangular slopsieve and rinsing them, working the pump handle with an easy regularity, two dogs at her feet and a cat on the counter all waiting to be fed.

"Click!" he said. His two hands were raised, forming a rectangle with fingers and thumbs. "Country girl at pump. Pretty as a picture. . . ."

She turned around and he stopped grinning. Her face was white and there were circles under her eyes.

"You feel as bad as you look?"

She shrugged. "Planning to work today?"

"I was thinking of it."

"I figured you might."

Her tone was neutral, but there was something else hanging in the air. He couldn't quite place it.

"Have a bad night?"

"Good beginning," she said with a ghostly little smile. They had agreed to abstain during her first three months, but they hadn't been able to stick to it. "So now the stomach's acting up. Retribution."

"I can get my own eggs."

"Relax." She poured his coffee from the kettle which simmered at the back of the old wood-burning range. He sipped it while she put eggs in the frypan. The room was as quiet as it ever was—just the sound of the wood fire, the sizzle of hot fat in the pan, the scratching of a dog, the rustling of the guinea pigs in their cage next to the stove.

"Something's eating you," he said.

"Huh."

"Something's knotted up in there. What's the trouble?"

A weary little smile and then she lifted the egg off the hot iron, flipping it over. "Can't a girl have any privacy?"

"Like that blister?"

When they were in college they had taken a four-day hike in the wilds of Baxter State Park. She had come down from the peak of Mount Katahdin without complaining about a blister which had already become infected. Later, she almost lost the toe.

"Erik, how about staying home today?"

He set his mug down hard. "Stay home? When I've been sitting on my butt all winter? Aren't you tired of looking at my ugly face day after day?"

He was grinning, but he didn't feel it. Did she think he went down there and froze his hands scraping and painting in an unheated boat yard just for fun?

She scraped the eggs out of the pan and slid them onto a plate without blotting the oil off with a paper towel the way she usually did. Her face and the tired carelessness of her movement startled him.

"Look," he said, "how about this? How about if I take the kids?"

"To the yard?"

"To the yard. I'll put them to work."

"Yuh. O.K."

No protest. Not even thanks. She went back to the sink and he ate in silence. The eggs were leathery.

The trip to the boat yard was surprisingly quiet. The boys had worn themselves out feeding and currying the four goats, and they were impressed at being hired as helpers at the yard.

"Will they pay us?" Michael asked.

"*I* will."

"How much?"

"Twenty cents an hour for you and ten for Timmy."

"That doesn't seem like very much." This from Timmy.

"You're just starting out. Life's hard when you're just starting out."

And there it rested. The boys really didn't have any choice. They rode in silence, three men going to work.

The route was mostly by back roads. It took them through small clusters of weathered and tar-papered shacks surrounded by rusting auto bodies, broken lobster traps, spare lumber, battered dories, baby carriages filled with kindling—nothing expendable in this harsh land.

"What's that?" Timmy asked. There was something quite bloody in the road ahead.

"Probably a fox," Michael said from the back seat with the annoying assurance of an older brother. He had been curled up in fetal comfort in a clutter of brown-stained drop cloths. Now he leaned forward with interest.

"Tail's not big enough," Erik said. Its head had been mashed, but the rest of it looked rather like a woodchuck. He slowed up, partly to swing clear of it and partly to see it better.

"Poor little fox," Timmy said. His tone was one he reserved for dead mice, dead flies, and even ants. Erik found this vaguely disturbing. Shouldn't the boy be out trapping and skinning animals at his age? It was hard to know; he had no measure with which to judge what a country boy should be doing.

"Save your pity," he said. "He had to go sometime. That way's as good as another."

"Yuch!" Michael said.

"What do you mean, 'yuch'?"

"Well, *I* wouldn't want to go that way—just like a thing."

"You wouldn't know what hit you."

They drove on in silence for a few moments. Erik gripped the wheel, angry at himself for reasons he couldn't place. There were times when he said things to the boys he didn't really believe and that didn't make any sense to him. It was as if they drove him to it.

"Daddy," Timmy said, "couldn't we go back and give it a funeral?"

"It's a dead goddamned *thing* in the road. What's the matter with you?"

That killed the conversation. They drove the rest of the way in silence.

By the time they reached the boat yard, the incident had been forgotten. As soon as they turned onto the old, pitted, dirt road, the boys started jumping in their seats, exaggerating the bumps in the road and laughing. Erik swerved unnecessarily on the curves, joining the joke.

When he caught sight of the old gray sheds and the cold shimmer of the bay beyond, he found himself looking for other cars. There were none. Most of the men avoided Sunday work. He felt a twinge of regret. For an instant he had imagined arriving with two lanky adolescents, shaggy haired, slouching, and good natured. Erik and his boys, all members of that kindly, shabby group who spent their days scraping and caulking and painting.

But the illusion was broken by their shrieks of delight at those bumps in the road. He pulled to a stop by the main shed with more abruptness than was necessary. His sons had altogether too much exuberance. And they were too verbal. He wished they were more like the boys who went lobstering, low-keyed, given to wry comments delivered straight-faced. *They* never jumped in their seats or shrieked like that, not even at four. They had been hardened in a way his own had not—in a way *he* had not.

"O.K. now," he said sharply as soon as they were in the chill twilight of the main shed, "if you're old enough to work, you're old enough to remember a few basic rules." Both boys looked at him soberly. "You stick to your own work, right? If you take a break, just let me know and then rest. No wandering off and climbing on other boats. And a couple of other things. No teasing, no complaining. Keep your eyes on your work. And don't keep chattering away. You boys talk too much."

The boys nodded solemnly, and they began opening and mixing

paints. It was an old lobster boat they were working on—a large, scruffy vessel but proudly equipped with a converted Chrysler engine, eight cylinders, and over $6,000 worth of electronic gear.

Erik felt a reverence for such boats. Each one represented a lifetime of work. Most of the lobstermen had started with open dories powered by outboards and year by year worked toward something they could take pride in. Erik's starting point was land based, the Nubian goats. Four so far and one pregnant. He had land for grazing and new markets for the fur, the milk—used in yogurt—and the animals themselves as pets. All it would take was an agony of work.

For a while, the boys worked quietly and steadily. Erik stayed above them, painting the decks a utility gray. The boys remained on the ground below, assigned to the red-copper bottom paint. There was a good margin for error there; and Timmy, too young for real work, could pretend to be doing his part. Erik could finish that side later.

It was just as well that the other workers were not down that day. Theirs was an easy, close fraternity of men who had gone to school together. Erik was still the outsider. They respected his strength and his willingness to work, but they were uneasy about a man who raised goats and sold yogurt to summer people. "How's things on the Musk Ox Farm?" they would ask as if Erik and his family were themselves some slightly odd herd. His boys, not yet fully broken to work, would not have been appreciated.

At the end of the second hour, the complaints began to mount. What time was it? How much longer would it take? How come the paint was so drippy? He held his temper, but he wondered how long it would be before they would stay with a job.

"Lunch break," he said, and there were exaggerated groans of relief. "Come on now, you've only put in two hours." He climbed down the ladder to help Timmy wrap his brush in newspaper. He watched Michael out of the corner of his eye, pleased that his eldest was willing to imitate the ritual without being instructed.

He would have preferred to eat down by the shore—the sun made it warmer outside than in. But the boys wanted to eat in the cockpit and they needed some reward.

Erik opened his can of beer and leaned against a pile of life pre-servers, ropes, and tarpaulins stained red with bottom paint. He drew his knees up under his chin to rest his back. Looking aft he could see a kind of trail in the dirt floor where the skids under the cradle had been dragged last fall. Soon—the next day, perhaps—they would move the cradle back again along that same path, easing it with cables, prying it this way and that with crowbars, old Skol-field cursing without anger, nudging it until it was on the tracks which led from the door down to the sea. This was the part that Erik liked—sweating under the directions of the old master, a distant rel-ative by marriage, responding to terse directions—"ease her an inch thisaway. . . . I didn't mean no inch-and-a-quarter." Up from the sea in the fall, down again in the spring. The yard had been built in the Civil War and that rhythm—a six-month tide—had been repeated for over a hundred years.

"Well," he said, coming back to the task at hand, "lunch time is over. Back to work."

"So soon?" Michael asked.

"So soon," he said. "Let's get this over with quickly. Your mother doesn't like being left home all alone on a Sunday. Neither would you."

"But I'm not a grownup."

"Grownups don't change *that* much. Think you can finish with that bottom paint in an hour or so?"

"Jees." Michael's enthusiasm was flagging; Timmy's was gone.

"This isn't any fun," he said.

"So who promised fun? Do you think *I* come down here for fun? Listen," he said, again on the edge of rage, "this has to be done. Are you old enough for it or not?"

They all went back to work in silence. There was no way of telling how they felt about it. He didn't really want to know. Besides, he had given them a choice, hadn't he?

He threw himself into brute effort. Mindless, he moved the brush as rapidly as it would go without splattering. His arm and back ached, but it would all be worth it. If he was going to be known as the grubber, he might as well earn the title.

There had been times when he had been put down for that, of course. Like the previous week when he was varnishing masts outside, moving fast, and old Skolfield gave him hell. "No sense to that. Stop and look up." The sky was purple-black with rain clouds. "Any fool could see it's going to rain and ruin everything you've done there. You work like a grubber, you do. A man's got to look up once in a while."

Well, that was an exception. Most of the time it paid to get the job done. Right now he had finished the deck and moved down into the cockpit. If he could complete that before the end of the day, they could launch her at high tide the following noon, a day before promised. There would be satisfaction in that.

When the squall hit, he was caught by surprise.

"Damn it to hell!" Timmy's voice from outside. And then thunk! like a brush being slapped against the hull. Again, *thunk!*

Erik scrambled up out of the cockpit and jumped to the ground without even touching the ladder. "Watch it," he shouted. "No paint slinging in this yard. What's going on?"

"It keeps *drip*ping," he wailed and deliberately whacked the wet paint again.

Erik's temper snapped with that third slap of the brush. It was a goddamned tantrum, that's what it was. He charged at his son, head lowered like a bull. "Didn't I just tell you. . . ."

The boy was eye-wide terrified, but he held his ground. His face was streaked with dirt, tears, and red paint; he was a tiny savage in bloody war paint.

Erik stopped, put his hands on his hips, stared down at Timmy, and laughed.

"Hail, Timothy," he said, "King of the Pygmies."

The boy's paintbrush struck him hard on the left cheek, an inch below his eye.

In the nightmare which followed there were no clear pictures. Somehow he had got the boy jammed down over his knees to spank his rear, and over the howling there was another child yelling and beating him about the shoulders and neck like a mother bird. And at some point the other child got his thrashing too, cries echoing as if in a cave, sending a flock of outraged pigeons wheeling out from the rafters.

The trip home was as silent as a funeral. It was perfect idiocy, he decided, trying to shape them in the image he wanted for himself. His own father had been a distant figure, working at the hardware store all day and caring for the books evenings and even some weekends. He was hard on himself and others. Once in a long while, the old man would loosen up enough to talk. Usually it was about his childhood, his life on the farm which in retrospect he made sound ideal. All the good values were back there. But these were such rare moments—how could Erik learn from those how to be a father? These boys made him feel brutish, clumsy, and irascible.

On the way home he stopped at a general store and bought a Popsicle for each of the boys. They muttered thanks and he started the Jeep and continued on their way.

"Aren't you having any?" Michael asked.

"I don't feel like eating."

Michael held out his Popsicle stick. "Here," he said. "Have a bite."

Erik took a bite for the ritual of it. Then Timmy, with a nudge from his brother, made his offering. Erik accepted that too.

When at last they drove down their own muddy road, past the family cemetery, and around the barn, they were talking about the goats and what the billy did to get the nanny pregnant, and how they would market the fur, and how the place would one day support them all without his having to find outside work, how they would share it, and, yes, how there would be a time when the boys would be running it themselves. It was marvelous how often they could listen to all that when they were in the mood.

Pulling to a stop by the house, he noticed that the wind had shifted to the north, coming in hard and cold. He also saw fabric draped over the juniper bushes. It reminded him of the wisps of musk ox hair they used to find when they first moved there. But no, it was clothing. The laundry—she hadn't bothered to use clothespins, hadn't even finished the rest of the load. Shirts, sheets, and pillow-cases were scattered in the tall grass. What he had first seen in the juniper was a pair of her panties. Incredibly careless.

"Damn her," he said aloud. If he was willing to care for children for a whole afternoon couldn't she finish a simple job?

"You play outside," he said to the boys. He went inside, slamming the door behind him. She was not in the kitchen or the living room.

"Sal," he called.

"Upstairs."

He charged up, shaking the house. He found her in bed, listening to music from the portable radio, a cat curled up beside her. In bed in the middle of the day? Her maternal privilege, perhaps, but not his image of her.

"The laundry's all over the yard," he said.

"I've had it," she said.

"*You've* had it! Wait 'till I tell you about *my* goddamned day."

"I mean the baby."

He took a deep breath. "Here? Alone?"

She nodded, pointing to the floor beside the bed without looking down. There, surrounded by dark-stained towels and torn sheeting, was the chamber pot. And in it, curled and bloody, was his child. It was about as long as his own thumb. He knelt down.

She was saying something. Repeating it. "Erik, is it a boy or a girl?"

"Never mind that. What about you? Are you bleeding?"

"I'm all right, I guess. It's stopped. But the laundry's blowing all over the hillside. I had to leave it."

"To hell with the laundry." How could she be thinking about that when her whole being should have been filled with rage against what had happened. No, rage against *him*. He had left her alone—no car and no phone. And there had been signs. "Any fool could see it." Skolfield's words. Crazy for work, he'd gone and ruined everything.

Spending his day midwifing a goddamned boat! Was he blind as
well as brutal?

"My fault," he muttered, laying his head on the edge of the bed.
"The whole idea." He meant coming to live there in the first place.
Trying to make the land work for them. He had made a brute of
himself. Even the boys had more sensitivity than he, wanting to bury
that miserable thing in the road. No wonder men had abandoned the
farms, blunted by the agony of effort. Brutalized.

"A killing place. It's turned into a killing place."

His eyes filled with tears for the first time since childhood. He had
hold of her arm. He had led her into this and now he would have to
lead her out again. They would have to start looking for a new life all
over again.

"*Not* a killing place," she said.

"I killed it."

"Don't be stupid. Listen, we shouldn't be saying 'it.' We should
find a name which could be either." He looked at her, amazed, but
she went on. "Like Robin, maybe. It's a spring name. And I've been
thinking—could we bury him or her in the cemetery? With a little
stone? Some kind of marker."

"O.K.," he said gently, "but you hush up now. Get some rest." He
wasn't following her. It sounded morbid to him. It wasn't good to be
talking like that.

"I've *been* hushed up all afternoon," she said gently. "I've had
time to think. That's our cemetery too, now. I was thinking, maybe
we could fix up the other stones. Set them up. Fence it. And let the
goats crop the plot. Keep it trim. I like that, having the goats keeping it trim. And . . . hey, don't look at me as if I'm sick. I'll be O.K.
tomorrow. Can you do my chores this afternoon?"

He nodded. "Stupid question."

"Don't forget the laundry."

"Laundry first. Then milking the goats."

"Yes, the goats. And feeding the dogs."

"There's a fish head for the cat."

"Hamburger for the four of us?"

"Hamburgers, and we still have three jars of our own beets. You know, we did all right last winter. Three jars left and it's spring already."

In a great flooding of gratitude he lay his shaggy head on her stomach. Instinctively she winced, but there was no need to; he rested it there with a new gentleness, weightless with compassion. Touching her there, he felt in the same instant a remorse for the dead and a new, trembling love for the living.

Bruno in the Hall of Mirrors

Bruno was in his old familiar sleeping bag again. He realized this even before opening his eyes. He liked the feeling of the coarse wool against his hairy legs. *Sleeping bag*? What the hell had happened? It had been months since he had camped out. He played with the problem of where he might be, knowing that all would be explained as soon as he opened his eyes—a peek-a-boo game with reality.

But when he did look it was clear that Reality, the bitch, had cheated. He was lying in a desert, a goddamned moonscape. From his retina to the horizon there was nothing but jagged hunks of rubble. Moon, earth, or dream, it was a ruination. And he had to urinate. He wondered if, under the circumstances, there was any reason why he shouldn't let go right there in his bag.

"Oh crap," he said aloud. The incantation broke the spell. The doors to reality swung open and he was lying in the middle of the floor of his apartment in New York with shafts of morning sun beaming down through the filthy windows.

Lying in the middle of the floor? Who in hell took all the furniture? He sat up abruptly and woke Sara, tugging at her hair. "Take a look at that," he said.

The two of them sat there: naked, massive Bruno with simian fur covering the breadth of his chest; and lean, long-boned Sara, small-breasted and tight-muscled as an adolescent. They were dazed and fascinated—like spectators at a fatal accident.

"That Enrico," he said at last.

"That dear bastard," she said—"dear" because he was an old friend, jolly and fat; and "bastard" because as a sub-tenant for three months he had stripped the place and used it as a sculpture studio. Broken pieces of abstract frescoes were all that remained, more fragmentary even than the rubble of Pompeii.

Bruno and Sara had made the initial discovery late the previous night. They had seen the ruination by matchlight because the electricity had been shut off. But they had been too exhausted to react fully then. They had slept numb like returning refugees.

As she leaned forward to scratch her leg, her shoulder brushed his. He was reminded that all was not lost. Sara was very much there beside him. It was a pattern they had begun when he was at Columbia and had continued when he cut out and went to Georgia. But for the past three months he had been in a county jail down there and she, necessarily, could not be with him. Now he had her back and had lost all his furniture. O.K., he thought, to hell with furniture.

She pulled a pack of crumpled cigarettes from the pocket of his pants, which she had used as a pillow, and lit one for him. As she was doing this, he rubbed the side of his leg against hers.

"All this dust," he said, "leaves me itchy."

"We've been living in itchy dust for three months," she said.

He took the cigarette from her and she did the rubbing.

"Next time," he said, "let's share a cell."

"Next time let's run."

They rocked back and forth together, talking softly. And by the time their cigarette was finished they were half out of the bag, rolling together in the rubble, laughing and coughing and raising a cloud of white dust like smoke, as if they had once again caught fire in the middle of that enormous ash-heap of a room.

Reclamation began there. Later they showered and dressed and shoveled and finally swept out the place, sprinkling the floor to keep the dust down. They borrowed a mattress from the old Latvian in the basement and lined up a friend of a friend who said he thought he could help them get some of the furniture back.

Not that any of it was worth worrying about. The bed, for example, was of no special value to them. The Latvian's faded mattress was just as good, and it gave the old man a chance to "do a favor for a fellow Slav," Bruno's father being a Czech. And they preferred to sit on the floor rather than on chairs. But she didn't like the way the room echoed without her Iranian prayer rug on the floor, and he missed his Coltrane records and his books—particularly the ones on medieval civilization and alchemy. They weren't the sort you could pick up in the corner drugstore.

They had taken turns going out for sandwiches, cigarettes, coffee, and to make phone calls—it was important not to miss whoever it was who was going to help them find their belongings. But there was no need for all that. He didn't show up until evening.

Bruno had lit the gas log and added a couple of candles for light and the two of them were on the mattress munching on a pre-barbecued chicken and sipping Punt e Mes when the door to the hall swung open. The figure was silhouetted against the glare of the hall light behind him.

"You the Bruno?" The accent was Spanish.

"I'm not the Christ child," Bruno said mildly. "You're the one who has our things?"

"I'm Pesos." As he swung the door shut behind him they could see him by candlelight. He was a tall, thin Puerto Rican with Victorian sideburns. He wore a suede, hip-length jacket belted at the waist. "Pesos—that's like 'two bits' in Spanish." He grinned and a gold tooth glistened in the golden light. "No, I don' have your stuff. But I take you where you find it."

"Where's that?" Sara asked.

Pesos shoved his hands deep into his coat pockets and made an exaggerated long face. "Waal, you might say it's here and there. So to speak.

"Did he sell it or give it away?" Bruno said, biting into a drumstick.

"Like you might say, lent it away, man. Lent it away." He gestured broadly and Bruno pictured Enrico, round and cheerful, going up and down Grand Street, passing out books, chairs, pillows in the little Kosher meat markets, in the Hebrew Men's Club, and to the Italian kids who swept into the district for stickball. His vision was a grand tableau of generosity and brotherhood . . . that dear bastard.

Pesos squatted down and accepted a chicken wing. He also tried the wine but made a face with the first sip and wouldn't take more.

"You mad at Enrico maybe?" he said, munching.

"I should bash his head in," Bruno said, but he kept tight rein on his tone. During those six months in Georgia—half of them in jail—hatred had sifted down on him like fallout. It had almost reached his marrow. He'd be damned if he was going to stir up more at this point.

"An artist," Pesos said, his mouth full of chicken, "is not like people. He has special needs. And, waal, he needed space here. So several of us help him make space."

"Thanks a lot," Sara said, taking a gulp from the wine bottle.

"But I make it up to you. I have a truck outside. We'll pick up the stuff."

On the way down the stairs Bruno felt lightheaded—partly the wine and partly dislocation. He kept thinking that New York would snap into focus, that places and people would become familiar again. The process was taking longer than he had expected. His dear friends had stolen more from him than just furniture. He climbed into the battered old truck and sat between Pesos and Sara. With the three of them lined up in the dark like that, he half expected some ham-handed, red-faced deputy to tell them to hand over their belts, wallets, and watches. There were, he decided, a lot of loose and frayed wires slatting about in his head.

Pesos drove with an easy abandon, the old stake-body truck shuddering at each shift in course. He talked about two new theaters which had opened off Broadway and some of the plays that were planned, but his words glanced off Bruno. He couldn't care less about all that. Theater was a bore. Somewhere, scattered about in the enormous city, were bits and pieces of himself. The search for them was important.

For a while they were blocked by a trailer truck trying to back into a warehouse, and Pesos took a hand-rolled cigarette out of a little tin box. "Panama Red," he said, lighting it carefully. "For my frans." They passed it back and forth, inhaling deeply, watching the huge trailer being inched forward and back, being lined up for the penetration. Bruno grinned at the enormity of it. Here was Hollywood's idea of a daring symbolic detail. He himself took no symbol seriously—not even the candlelit icons of his father's Orthodox church. As far as he was concerned, the more gross the symbol, the more comic it was. He closed his eyes and wished he were back in his nonsymbolic sleeping bag with Sara.

The time machine slipped its clutch noiselessly and he found himself walking through dark canyons which might have been Cooper Village, the three of them holding hands, swinging arms, and Bruno delivering a little discourse on the rustic charm of villages like Cooper.

"A return to the simple virtues of the eighteenth century," he heard himself saying. "Sturdy wives drawing water from the town well; menfolk out toiling in Central Park; a bronzed and hardy people confronting unspoiled nature. Oh to be raised in Cooper Village."

Somehow they floated to an upper floor—stairs? an elevator? gossamer wings?—and were confronting a Danish couple who wore matching black-rimmed glasses. Pesos was saying something to them about a hot plate, a kitchen table, some dishes, pans, and books. Bruno watched them while the walls of the apartment billowed pleasingly like a backdrop painted on silk.

"Is it truly necessary to have them back?" the man asked.

"You Americans," the woman said, "have the love only for *things*."

Bruno had been paying attention with only half a lobe. He was much more concerned with a view into the next room. Potted palms and philodendrons and hanging vines basked in neon sunlight and across the white-tiled floor came an enormous, jet black cat with yellow eyes. There was something in her deliberate steps which reminded him of Sara walking barefoot in the early morning.

"I'll take my *things*," he said, speaking pleasantly but distinctly and hearing his voice from afar, "or I'll take your cat and hold her ransom."

"You'd better do what you're told," Sara said. "He's a cat molester."

So they won that skirmish and piled the table and chairs and lamps into the back of the truck, together with a clutter of Pesos' things already there—a moose's head, a stage flat depicting trees and a meadow in the distance, and a naked mannequin. Bruno shook hands with the mannequin, patted his or her bottom, and then slid into the cab beside Sara and they glided off into the dark again.

"Where was the cat?" Sara said. "I didn't see any cat."

"It was a beautiful cat," Bruno said.

"A tiger in the jungle," Pesos said.

"With big, golden eyes," Sara said.

And they were at a town house on Waverly Place where a fat doctor was entertaining a gray-blond woman who spoke only German. She was particularly reluctant to give up a carved wooden jewel case, a Czechoslovakian treasure (without contents) which Bruno's father had bought for his wife at the 1939 World's Fair. It was all the family had "from the old country," and Bruno was sure it had been made in a Brooklyn sweatshop. Over the years the damn thing had been metamorphosed into a holy ark. It had finally been given to Bruno by his dying mother, part gift and part curse. Bruno hated it but he didn't like the way the gray-blond Brunhilde held on to it, fingering the carvings acquisitively.

Pesos had a list and was reading items from it: two chairs, plastic curtains, a clothes hamper, an electric iron, a bird cage with two starlings in it, a mobile made with rusty nuts and bolts, a lobster kettle. . . . Pesos wandered through the doctor's apartment gathering these things while their host stood there, gargling with Germanic oaths.

He was demanding something about proof of ownership, and

when the woman asked him in German what was going on, he shouted back at her in German as if she were one of the conspirators. Finally he turned to Bruno.

"You have no right over these things." His face was red. "You come in here as a stranger. You're looting my home! You want me to call the police?"

Then, abruptly, he shrugged as if facing a hopeless injustice and said, "Take them." So without another word they did, and Bruno barely remembered the actual transporting. Somehow they were down on the street again and slithering through the city, the truck now elevated from the pavement like a silent hovercraft. Pesos began singing "Silent Night, Holy Night," and they all joined in.

The craft hove to and lingered there a moment in the dark, bobbing gently and swaying with the tide.

"We now have some of your things," Pesos said. "Am I right?"

"You are right," Bruno said. "You are so right."

"Waal, the rest is not so easy."

"What rest?"

"The living room stuff, man. The living room. It's all at one place. Like it's being used right now."

"Let's un-use it," Sara said.

"Not so easy."

Bruno, though still at sea, smelled fraud in the air. He told Pesos that, and Pesos was hurt at the lack of trust.

"My fran, I brought you some things. The rest I cannot get tonight. But I can show you where it is. Would you like that? I show you that it exists and then later—another day—we talk about how to get it. Agreed?"

Bruno clenched his right hand into a fist. It wasn't anger—he just wanted to see something solid for a change. He placed his other hand over the knot of flesh and bone, like a ball-and-socket joint. Holding his own fist like that in the dark was reassuring—like gripping an altar rail—or the horizontal bar in the county jail cell.

How extraordinary, he thought, that he had been in that Georgia jail on the morning of the previous day. Time was altogether too elastic. He could still hear the sound of breakfast forks and knives scraping against their metal food-trays, the bench-scraping and coughs and belchings of a hundred men forbidden speech, the squawks of the rubber squeegies as they swabbed down the concrete floors. He could feel the dead weight of boredom. He could smell the faintly sulfurous scrambled eggs, the rancid fats from the kitchen, the Lysol of the latrine, the beautiful pine-tree odor of the carpentry shop. All these were with him, vivid and immediately present: but the experience itself had slid back until it was almost vicarious— some *other* Bruno Zelek had quit college and joined the Freedom School in Georgia and had strayed from teaching to direct action and had ended up in jail on a crazy charge of insurrection; and now *he* was one of those moral voyeurs who could read the paper and pay tribute to the splendid work of that young idealist without taking as much as a single step toward danger *and it was an enormous relief.*

"I'm out," he said aloud. "Out." It was as if he had just that moment been sprung. He clapped his great fist against the flat of his palm.

"An' baby, you're *in*," Pesos said. "Like you know that, don' you?"

"Out," Bruno said. "That's all I care about."

"He's *in*," Pesos said to Sara. "Picture in the papers. Everyone knows his name."

"A lot of good that did," Sara said.

"Big rally too. Lots of speeches."

"Wish we'd been here. Instead of there."

"An' spoil everything?"

Bruno let their voices slip out of focus and watched the dark succession of doorways and loading platforms slide past them, noiseless as a waterfront on a moonless night. The air was fluid and his mind swirled gently in eddies.

It was marvelous how many tall-masted cranes stood next to half-dismantled buildings. It seemed to Bruno that they were stripping the city and perhaps preparing for a new show. The night was intermission time and in the morning he would wake and. . . . He stared at still another crane and another building in rubble and another couple locked together in the shadow of a rusting truck. *Another couple?* Hell, it was the *same* couple there. Pesos must have been circling. How many times had they been by the same scene? He turned questioningly to Pesos and saw him squinting at his watch. They were stopped again and Pesos' hands were at the top of the wheel and he was trying to read the time.

Odd, Bruno thought. Time had been so free-flowing all evening and Pesos so loose—why the change? They were passing under a streetlight now and again Pesos studied his watch. His face was drawn, a different person altogether. They they swung into a dead-end alley only wide enough for one car and stopped at a loading platform.

"Here," Pesos said. They all got out without asking any questions. They climbed upstairs to a warehouse door.

"You must keep quiet," Pesos said to them. "No questions no matter what."

One question would have been why Pesos had a key to this place, but that was only one of many. And none were allowed. Silently they entered—hallway long and dark, one sooty bulb at the end of a cord, plaster cracked to the lath, an unenclosed pay phone with a black halo of names and numbers on the wall around it, floorboards squealing at every step. And from out of a doorway down at the end stepped a man in a cape and Pesos said, "Ho kay?" and the stranger, "Wait," and they waited.

"Crazy," Sara said. "This whole bit."

But what else could one add? They waited in silence. Bruno smelled plaster dust and sweat. Then he heard music. It was a chorus. Good God, it was "Onward Christian Soldiers"! He started to ask about this but was hushed. Then the other man was ready for them and Pesos told Sara to wait there for just a minute. Bruno was ushered down the hallway feeling vaguely sick and humming "Onward Christian Soldiers."

The stranger and Pesos led Bruno up a few steps, holding onto his arms as if he were a condemned prisoner taking the last walk. The music grew louder. They were passing some heavy draperies and Pesos whispered, "When we let go of your arm, turn right and keep walking. Go right in where the stuff is and make sure it's all there. Just check it over. But don't say a thing."

"Or," the other one said, "you'll never get your furniture back." It was a line out of a kidnapping movie. He, Bruno, was supposed to answer, "*You wouldn't dare,*" his voice trembling. But his throat was dry and the words stuck as if he had stagefright.

"Now!" Pesos said, and they gave him a little shove. He turned right and stumbled into a lighted room. He kept walking as they had told him to and then stopped still. He was right back in his own living room. It was furnished now. Everything was there. . . .

His couch—the flush door and foam rubber type covered in black with a patch in gray—and the red sling chair and the cinderblock-and-board bookcases and even his own books and magazines scattered in his own disorderly order. And on top of a stack of magazines was the Coltrane album which he remembered playing all night before taking the bus for Georgia. It had a torn cover. And on the floor, the Iranian prayer rug. The entire room was exactly as he had left it. Except for that insane music. And except for a bearded stranger sitting on his couch reading a copy of *Encounter*. He didn't even look up. He just sat there reading.

Bruno swayed, caught himself, and ran his hand through his hair. He squinted, trying to focus. Was he really obliged to say nothing? Then over the sound of the music there was the screech of a World War I whistling bomb coming down on them. He held his breath. Just before the explosion he turned around and looked out past a glare of lights and saw an entire theater of people watching him. He opened his mouth to say "A stage!" when the bomb hit thunderously and the curtain fell.

The explosion and music gave way to a storm of applause and cheering from behind the curtain.

He stood there dumbly, feeling like a Kodiak bear who has been tricked into performing at a shoddy circus. For a moment he considered ripping at the curtain. Behind it, the applause splattered like hail.

Then from the wings a variety of people materialized: a round hunk of a man in a black corduroy shirt, the Danish couple with black-rimmed glasses, a fat man resembling Enrico, two beautiful black girls, Pesos, the German doctor, and others. They all lined up with their arms across each other's shoulders. Bruno was half a head taller than any of them, but they managed to lock him into the center of the row. The curtain rose. The lights blasted him. The applause swelled and the line of which Bruno was now a part bowed low, bending him with it. He tried resisting, but it was as if the weight of the entire cast was on his shoulders and so he had no choice. When the curtain fell for the third time the line broke and the chunky man with the black shirt seized Bruno by both shoulders.

"Well done!" he said, giving Bruno a little shake. "Just what we had in mind." He turned to Pesos, smiling like a circus manager. "And for once you didn't muff it. Good timing, Pesos."

There was a flurry of activity as everyone pressed to shake Bruno's hand. It was splendid, they told him. Couldn't have been better. His expression. That gesture of running his hand through his hair. Magnificent. That look of alarm. Was he *sure* he hadn't rehearsed it? Had he never been on the stage before?

Bruno stood there, slowly turning from one to the other. The black-shirted ringmaster was introducing him now, but there was no way of connecting the right bodies with the names. He kept nodding at the wrong face and the chorus would repeat "No, no, not that one," and laugh and turn him in the right direction as if he was about to pin the tail on a donkey.

The two solemn Danes from Cooper Village peered up at him, their eyeglasses flashing like headlights. "A striking *event*," they told him. Behind them was the German doctor. How did *he* fit into all this? "Very natural," he said, clapping Bruno on the back. "Very unaffected. Did you never guess? Not even at the end?"

"Guess what?" Bruno asked, surprised that they hadn't taken his voice as well.

"Marvelous, marvelous," the thin, bearded one said, raising his arm and letting his hand drop down limp at the wrist like the head of a dead duck. "Oh you are *too* perfect."

A tall Negro in a white shirt opened the curtains again. Most of the audience had left the tiny theater, but a few lingered by the back row—a covey of teeny boppers, an old wino, a well-dressed couple. Some of those on the stage hopped down onto the floor, and some of those by the exit wandered up to the stage. The interchange was confused, but most everyone seemed to know each other.

Bruno had difficulty focusing on the scene until he found himself looking right into the fat face of Enrico—Enrico the thief, Enrico the violator of friendships and trust. *That* much was clear.

"You sonofabitch," Bruno said. It was a relief to be angry. With pleasure he grabbed Enrico's shirt front and lifted until his victim, red-faced now, was standing on the tips of his fat little toes. "Stole everything didn't you?"

"Oh, hey, Bruno, take it easy." He was having difficulty getting words out. "Peter, hey Peter, doll, tell him. Tell him about it before he kills me. Peter, hey Peter."

Peter turned out to be the blackshirt, and he was highly indignant. "What the hell is this?" he said. "You think you're an ape or something? Put him down." Bruno put him down, mainly because he was getting heavy. "I knew you wouldn't do the minute I set eyes on you. Wrong type. You're more of a wrestler than a pacifist."

"I'm no pacifist," Bruno said.

"Don't tell *me* what you aren't. This is *my* play, man."

He turned to the others and told them that there would be a five-minute break but to stick around for rehearsal and no one was to leave or he'd break their necks.

Once again he reached up and placed his two sweaty hands on Bruno's shoulders. His round head was set directly on a square hunk of a body. His blue-stubbled face looked up at Bruno with the chin-jutting confidence of a Mussolini.

"The play is mine," he said, this time with more pride than anger. "*I* wrote it. *I'm* producing it. And *I'm* directing it. That way there's no argument." He grinned at the mere thought of interference.

"I came to get my furniture back," Bruno said.

"And the name of this play—in case you haven't been reading the papers—is *The Saint of Saigon*." He swung his smile on his listeners like a searchlight, and they beamed back at him. "Actually Saigon is never mentioned in the play. The setting is Bruno's consciousness."

"Bruno?"

"Bruno." Peter gestured to the thin, bearded character who had been sitting on the couch reading *Encounter*. "We go by our role-names here, so he's Bruno day and night. Right, Bruno?"

"So right," the other Bruno said. "Abso*lute*ly." He turned to his namesake with a quiver of enthusiasm. "I even *dream* as Bruno."

"You can stay the hell out of *my* dreams," Sara said. She elbowed her way into the circle. "Come on," she said to Bruno, "let's get out of this freak house."

The crowd fell back as one might on discovering an uninvited guest.

"Who's the chick?" Peter asked.

"A friend of mine."

"Friend?"

"Friend."

"Friend like a bedmate?"

"Friend like it's none of your business."

"None of my business?" He paused for a moment, mouth open. "None of my business? It's *my* play. Didn't I just tell you? Like I'm running the show here. It's *my gig. My scene.* You dig?"

"I'm in if he's in," Sara said. "No one's going to lock me out again for a while."

"I'm not in," Bruno said.

"Of course you're in," Peter said. "You're Bruno, aren't you?" He plunged his stubby finger into Bruno's heart. "Look, man, I like your story. It's authentic. It's genuine. So I've gone to a lot of trouble getting this thing right. Enrico and me, we moved all your junk over here. We've spent hours poring over your journal and all those letters from your father—does he have rotten handwriting!—and I'm telling you I did a lot of revisions in the script. Like I wanted you to be more in the anti-war movement. I mean, that's the white scene right now. Tripping in the South ended in '63. You're out of phase. Like you're *nowhere* man. But I compromised. Me, Peter, compromised. I have you working *both* scenes. Peace and the race gig. For your story, I compromised. How's that for love?"

"Crap," Bruno said.

"Oh, *really*," the other Bruno said.

"Gratitude," Peter shouted, gesturing to everyone, "listen to that gratitude. For him we even held off the opening. We engineered a happening for the press. We sweated waiting for your arrival. And now we put our life's blood into rehearsals and open in two days and with what immortal words are we thanked by the man who claims sainthood? 'Crap.' Oh, such eloquence. Such nobility."

"Let them have it," Sara said. "Come on, love, let them have the junk and let's go."

"This is my room," Bruno, nee Bruno, said. "I mean, why the hell should I be thrown out of my own room?"

"*Well*," the other Bruno said, "we *are* being childish tonight, aren't we? I mean, *really*."

"Intermissions's over," Peter shouted. "Back to rehearsal." And to Bruno and Sara, "Enough clowning for now." He gestured them toward the audience. "Places everyone."

Sara started to leave and Bruno caught her by the wrist and brought her back. He sat down on the couch, arms folded. Sara sat beside him tentatively. Peter bellowed at the scattering of audience that they were to shut up, to stay in their seats, to put out cigarettes.

"You're crazy," Sara whispered to Bruno.

"It's my show. That's what they say."

"Like hell it's your show."

"Stick around. Maybe they'll give you a part."

"Good God, you're beginning to enjoy it!"

She started to get up and he pulled her down again. Peter had turned and was lecturing the actors. The other Bruno had been joined by a chorus of three Negroes—one man and two women. They were wearing black robes of the sort worn by Orthodox priests.

". . . so it's late and you're tired," Peter was shouting. "Forget it. You're going to move right into this the final scene. Forget everything else. Forget the little happening. It was only for kicks. Forget the audience. Pay no attention to these two clowns up here. Don't just play the part—*be* the *person*. In two days—Bruno, what happens in two days?"

Bruno started to open his mouth when the other Bruno supplied the words. "We open," he said.

"*Wrong*." Peter said, his voice thundering. "In two days we *become*. A transformation, not a play. A metamorphosis. A transmutation. A goddamned holy mass right here in this theater. Have you got it? Do you believe it?"

The other Bruno nodded. The chorus members took their cues from him and nodded too. Then Peter moved back into the wings where he stood, still visible, with the script in his hands.

For a moment there was utter silence in the darkened little theater. Then the other Bruno spoke, and with his words the final scene began.

"Get back," he said to the chorus. "Move back out of my life. You've no right to impinge so."

"We've come to stay," one of the girls said, her voice ringing with theatrical sincerity. "Wherever you wander, we'll be just behind you. In classes, in your father's apartment, in bed—always we'll be in your range of vision."

"But why me?"

"Because you've been chosen."

"But I can withdraw, can't I? I have rights, don't I?"

What interested Bruno was the way his namesake's voice and gestures were all exaggerated. It fascinated him. He wondered how he would do as an actor, and to find out he began miming each line. He did his best to use all his facial muscles and to employ gestures.

He was, he thought, doing quite well for an amateur, when someone in the audience began shouting—something about getting that bastard out of there. Bruno was not sure whom they meant.

"You must submit to your destiny," the chorus was chanting.

"But I wish to lead my own life."

"You have no life. Submit, submit. You must submit. . . .."

He noticed that under their robes the members of the chorus were barefooted—not at all like the priests of his childhood. The one speaking with the other Bruno was now directly in front of the couch but facing the audience. She had, Bruno thought, lovely feet and a long, graceful neck; and he was suddenly sure that except for the robe she was nude. It was, after all, hot under the lights.

"Let's go," Sara hissed.

On impulse, Bruno flipped up the back of the girl's robe. "Hey!" Sara shouted, and the girl spun and kicked him, her bare foot surprisingly painful, and the other Bruno was saying, "Oh, *really* now," and they were in a four-way fight, punching, pulling hair, and shouting. Then Bruno saw Sara leap from the stage and storm down the aisle toward the exit.

Once again he made the choice. He sprang free of the stage and ran down the aisle after her. When he got to the door, he knew that he would be able to catch her. She wouldn't run hard once she was outside. So he turned to catch one last glimpse of the play. They had resumed. The other Bruno was standing on the couch now while the chorus turned about him, chanting, and the wail of amplified saxophones filled the theater.

The strain of the evening finally hit Bruno and he felt the chicken and Punt e Mes come up with a resounding, hot rush. He barely had time to straighten up and wipe his mouth when the Danish woman with the glasses jumped from her seat and began shoving him back out the door.

"In the last act," she hissed. "You Americans have no pride. It's people like you," she added with a final thrust, "who ruin everything."

Greek Mysteries

The alarm clock had stopped. It must have. It read 1:33, and although that thick, sodden overcast probably still hung over all Greece as it had for twenty-two consecutive days, it certainly wasn't 1:33 at night.

By peering from under the coarse blanket, which was pulled high enough to keep his nose partially warm, Ernie could make out the kitchen chair on which the clock sat, the bureau with the sticking drawers which he and Madeline shared, and the corpse-white marble floor. This was another damn day, all right; but beyond that he knew nothing.

Instinctively he drew his arm up from under the covers—the cold air trickling down his neck like rainwater—to look at his wrist where his watch used to be. But then he remembered that it had stopped a month before, had been mailed back to New Jersey, and had never been heard of since. And their traveling clock had been forgotten in the chaos of packing—three months ago now. So how were the girls to get to school?

School! Good God, what about school? Of his three girls, two took a half-hour bus ride into the American School—Rachel in the ninth grade and Flick (the name somehow distilled from Felicia) starting out in kindergarten. The littlest, Trixie, was only four and stayed home. But the ritual of getting the girls ready by 7:30 and driving them out to the Government highway where the bus passed at 7:45

was all that kept the entire day from crumbling away at the very start.

"What time is it?"—Madeline's voice, muffled. She had taken to sleeping with her head entirely under the covers since coming to Greece. This was, he decided, very unlike her. She had also started sipping four or five retsinas before and during lunch and sleeping half of the afternoon while Trixie played next to the kerosene heater, scribbling with lipstick, tearing sheets or irreplaceable (everything was irreplaceable) bond paper into strips, pounding the keyboard of his typewriter to see all the little arms bunch together and make a tree.

There was a time when Madeline seemed to spend almost too much time with the children. He used to accuse her of meeting infants at their own level. It was hard, for example, to get her to follow a regular feeding schedule; she claimed she could sense their own inner rhythm—whatever that was. Of course it wasn't easy having two children only a year apart before she was twenty; and when he won custody of his Rachel that made three. It was, as Madeline liked to phrase it, instant family. Still, she did seem to be making progress.

But now—particularly since coming to Greece—she was withdrawing both from them and from him. These days she seldom smiled and sometimes he had to speak to her two or three times before she heard. He knew when he married her that it would take her time to mature, but he hadn't expected her to retreat. He wasn't quite sure how to deal with it either.

"I don't know," he said.

"Don't know what?" she mumbled.

"What time it is."

"What's the clock say?"

"One-thirty."

A pause. He thought she was asleep again. Then a thin, white hand curled around the edge of the blanket and pulled it down enough to reveal half a face. Brown eyes frowned at the room, at the day.

"It *can't* say one-thirty."

"It's stopped."

"Oh Jee-sus."

The head disappeared in a rush and the form under the blanket thrashed until it was halfway down to the foot and knotted up in a little ball.

Ernie felt a wave of resentment rise in his stomach like nausea. This clock failure was really her fault. He had been pacing around a good deal the night before and maybe he had kicked a chair or pounded the table when the subject of weather came up as it always did; but whatever the reason, she had urged more ouzo on him with some childish comment about floating above it all, and he did end up taking too much—not really drunk but just dulled and stupid. So he forgot to wind the clock. That simple. It was the first time he had forgotten since marrying Madeline six years before. It was a bad sign. He knew what it was to *really* fly high with a bottle and he wasn't going back to *that*. So he would have to tighten up a bit . . . one more twist on his own thumbscrews. For a starter he sat up in bed and let the cave-cold air work through to his skin.

There *might* still be time to get the girls to the bus. But he knew perfectly well that in this land of endless gray it also might be mid-morning. Or noon! It made him dizzy and a little sick to be so timeless. There were no fixed points. Even astronauts tumbling in outer space had fancy Omega watches to link them with the logic, order, and safety of earth-time.

"If we had a phone," he mumbled aloud, "I could call the school. If I knew a little more Greek I could find the village priest. Or listen to the radio. If the goddamned weather cleared for five minutes, we could look at the sun." It was a pointless, hopeless, liturgy. Some-how—through some outrageous miscalculation—he had caused his whole family to be swept overboard in mid-ocean; and now the old, familiar ship, moving steadily on a multitude of precise schedules, was only a distant throb and a mere smudge on the horizon. Ernie struggled against panic.

"Daa-dee! What time is it?"—this from Flick in the next room.

She was taking her first year in school very seriously and so woke with a sense of urgency.

"Don't know."

"Don't know? How come you don't know?"

The lump of blanket beside him was shaking gently and he wondered whether Madeline was laughing or crying. The odds were, he decided, about 50-50.

He heard a "swish-swish" approaching and Flick appeared through the curtain which separated the two rooms. Her bare feet were sliding over the snow-cold marble floor on two pieces of filthy burlap she had found in the road a month before. Somehow her white lambswool slippers had been left behind in New Jersey, and she preferred these burlap rags to whatever replacement they might have been able to find in the village.

With even less excuse, she draped her head and body in her gray army blanket rather than using her bathrobe. She pulled it around her each morning in the manner of old Greek widows. At the age of five she was already her own grandmother! It was clear that they were all going mad.

"How come you don't know?"

"The clock stopped," he said, dodging a public confession.

"Has the bus gone yet?"

"How in hell would I know? It might be dawn or it might be after-noon."

For once, Flick was caught without words. She stood there with her mouth slightly open. He hardly recognized her; she was an ad for the Save the Children Federation. If only he could shell out a ten-buck contribution and be done with it.

The curtain parted again and Rachel—the product of his first marriage—posed herself just behind her half-sister. Rachel at thirteen was a dark girl in every respect: long black hair, mahogany eyes, olive skin like her mother's, and moody as the old hag of Delphi. She slept in tight but crumpled Levi's and two bulky sweaters, the second of which had once been Ernie's and hung on her like a well-worn poncho.

"Why is Mother *hiding*?" she said in her Electra voice. He had forbidden her to call Madeline by her first name, but he couldn't train her to say "Mother" with warmth. Warmth? It was outlawed in this godforsaken country.

"She is not hiding," he said coldly. He had a sudden impulse to join Madeline under the covers, if only to avoid the eyes of the jury which now faced him. He had no real defense. At home back in New Jersey he, as an assistant professor of fine arts at Epsom College, owned a house with central heat, two separate baths with water that ran hot for the asking, two telephones, and the luxury of wooden floors, all of which he was renting to a colleague for less than he was paying here for this stucco tomb.

For the length of January, February, and March he had subjected his family to this bitter trial so that he could study and photograph samples of Byzantine art in rural, rarely visited churches. Initially, this expedition to purgatory had been excused by all on the grounds that minor Byzantine frescoes were his passion; but it was increasingly clear that he—already in his mid-thirties—was getting too old for passions. Life was work; there was no use pretending otherwise. Even Madeline—ten years his junior—was beginning to see that. When she married him she was only eighteen and she really believed with passionate enthusiasm that she could be a mother, a wife, and an honors student all at the same time. That was one myth that crumbled early. And then she upheld the delusion that his being on the faculty of Epsom College was something to be proud of. It took her some time before she understood why he insisted on calling the place by its former, humiliating name, Epson State Teachers College.

The last of the great myths to go was her husband's *passion* for Byzantine frescoes and icons. She was still reciting its tenets to faculty wives, students, and even the postman before they left. But after only three sleet-and-rain-filled weeks in the land of perpetual damp he overheard her in the other room saying firmly to Rachel, "Look, kiddo, your father *has* to finish that dissertation or he's *had* it." So there it was: the final myth dead from exposure; and in its place was the truth, naked and goose-fleshed.

"I'm hungry!" This was Trixie. At four she was the family's mascot. No one else's hunger would have been noticed. Standing there dirty-faced, with her father's rumpled suit jacket over her, sleeves touching the floor, she was one more reproach.

"All of you get dressed," Ernie said roughly, the firm master of the harem. And as if to release them from the spell of inaction he swung out of bed completely and, dressed in his Greek long johns and turtleneck jersey, stretched as if this were a normal morning with the prospect of a safe, orderly section of Fine Arts 101 to head for. With perfect stoicism he ignored the fact that his entire body from legs to jaws was quaking uncontrollably with the cold.

When he didn't hear anyone move he turned and faced them. Madeline had now come to the surface and, like the rest of them, was staring at him. Even the dog, Skili, had joined the family portrait. She was an untrainable, thoroughly stupid little black and white Greek mongrel, the replica of thousands of Greek mongrels, whose name, appropriately, meant "dog" in Greek. She stood there now with her head cocked, waiting for her master's voice.

"But what *are* we going to do?" Rachel asked. She didn't have to add, now that you've got us into this. It came across all right—like a radio beam through Arctic air.

"Do?" He was stalling. Any moment now the ragged little band would pick up their rifles and aim at his head. "Well, school is out of the question." If that won him points, they were keeping it secret. There were no whoops of delight such as he could evoke from college students by canceling a class. "So, I'm going to take the day off and we'll go for a picnic."

That did it. Flick and Trixie cheered and started chanting "A picnic, a picnic" and the miserable dog started yapping and the younger set trooped off to the other room. Rachel gave an exaggerated Greek shrug which was, she had once said, Camus in a single gesture; then she joined the others.

Only Madeline was left. She sat there in bed with her knees drawn up. Her brown hair was tumbled and the strands of her bangs were disordered as if she had been sailing on a windy day. For an instant he caught sight of what she was when he married her—a bright Radcliffe freshman, a potential fine arts major, daughter of an absurdly successful architect named Harry Bates, a townhouse resident of mid-Manhattan who summered in Maine. She seemed so undented. Mint fresh. And this meant a lot to Ernie, who was just then pulling his way up out of the chaos of a very bad marriage.

Now, only six years later, she seemed so shopworn and tired. It hardly seemed fair. He had put his share of sweat into the bargain— the most conscientious member of the department, even willing to teach in the summer to escape the charity of her father. Marriage to her was preceded by his full surrender to the academic world. And now, in spite of all this, she seemed incapable of sharing the burdens.

He wished right then she would say something girlishly cheerful about his plans for a picnic. Silently he put on his pants, wool shirt, two sweaters, and added the heavy socks to the ones he wore to bed. Why the hell didn't she speak?

"A picnic?" she said at last. She was talking into space, addressing it like a confidant. "A picnic in this weather? Out there on the tundra?" Now she turned to him. "Ernie, I think you are going— have gone, maybe—completely out of your mind."

Within a half-hour or an hour or perhaps two hours they had finished breakfast—or perhaps brunch—and rinsed out the dishes in cold water since there was no time to heat the big kettle. They had learned to do without cereal or eggs, starting the day with Greek bread and honey—the latter being very cheap if you remembered to bring your own jar or bottle to the store. This regional adjustment speeded breakfast considerably—time Madeline then spent mopping the white marble floor, which was always filthy after only one meal.

Fortunately she had just made a new jar of peanut butter. The ritual of shelling, skinning, and grinding the nuts, and adding the olive oil spoonful by spoonful—a recipe which she devised by experimentation—normally took an entire afternoon. But once made, it was easy to spread. Soon the sandwiches and olives and pickled octopus sections and the jug of retsina were packed in the Volkswagen bus. The two little girls and the dog provided some measure of enthusiasm. Flick kept asking about where they would go, what they would do, whether they could eat in a temple or see the place Daddy had been photographing. Trixie reported seeing sections of blue sky, but the bleating of those two high voices was so continuous that no one paid attention to them. When they were asked to put things in the car, they skipped and ran, making the dog yap and piddle her enthusiasm on the kitchen floor.

Rachel, on the other had, burned silently with a fearful flame. Her father was God only when he was steady and true to a cause. She had never quite forgiven him for giving up painting (when she was still living with her mother) and turning academic. Worse, he had come to Greece solely for the purpose of hammering out a dissertation. These were samples of decay; and the insistence on a picnic was proof of madness. The King had faltered in his rule and she was ready to finish him off in some grotesque rite from the *Golden Bough*. He could see it in her eyes.

He did his best to stay out of her way, but he didn't want to get within range of Madeline's muttering either. "When it starts raining," she was saying in a sing-song voice under her breath while spreading the sticky peanut butter, "we can all eat right in the car. Very cozy. A fun time. Let's see now, face cloth for the children; rags for the dog; retsina for us. Perhaps we can park on the government highway. Watch the convoys go by. The children could count the trucks. Oh it won't be so bad." All this with a kind of Ophelia-like cheerfulness.

They were out to get him. No question about that. But he would, damn it, impose a form on the day even without clocks. He would keep order. Actually he hated picnics—the lack of tables and chairs seemed somehow decadent—but it would serve as an activity. He had sailed enough to know that you can't steer if the boat stops its forward motion. They needed motion. After all, hadn't they asked him what to *do* that day?

Well, this was something to do. Vaguely he remembered some sea captain in a story by Conrad who sent his crew up into the rigging of a burned and sinking ship to furl the sails before the final descent. Only a man would understand that. And he was the only one present. Even that miserable dog was a bitch.

Once they were on their way, he took the back roads with no clear destination in mind. He had forgotten their only map, but he made a point of not mentioning that. He drove with fraudulent certainty, knowing only that it might be more picnic-like in the valleys to the south.

After what might have been an hour—he wished he knew—the road climbed through some low mountains and then, descending again, followed the general course of a small river. It crossed and re-crossed on narrow stone bridges. There were no villages here and not even houses. But, inexplicably, some of the hillsides were terraced for summer crops. The land here seemed to be more fertile than on the rocky hills where they had been living.

The little girls were with the dog in the way-back section over the motor. They had become strangely quiet. The high-voltage emotions of the morning—or whenever—seemed far behind them and somehow cut off by the growing height of these nameless mountains.

As they continued to descend with the river, the horizons rose further on either side of them. And in this long, sheltered valley the vegetation gradually became almost lush: grass stubble gave way to tall grains mixed with poppies and a variety of anemones. And there were real trees here. He hadn't realized how he had missed them back in the scrubby hillside village. Some of the wild fruit trees were just coming into bloom.

Still more amazing, further up the road and across another bridge there was actually a patch of sunlight.

"My God," Madeline said almost under her breath, "look at that."

"It won't last," Rachel said, leaning over from the seat behind.

"Right," Ernie said, anxious now to win points. "It'll be gone in a minute."

"Don't hex it," Madeline said.

"What's hex?" Trixie asked from the way-back.

"A spell. A curse," Madeline shouted back.

"Can Daddy really put a curse on the sun?"

"He can turn you into little pigs," Rachel said convincingly, "if you don't shut up."

Ernie twisted low, his cheek to the steering wheel, to squint at the sky and was amazed to see it in broken patches of blue. He felt an almost embarrassing flood of elation sweep through him—an emotion he hadn't felt since coming to Greece three months before. Three months?

"Madeline! It's April Fool's Day!"

"Are you sure?"

"Well, not exactly." Somehow the clock stopping had cut them off from calendar time as well. *Nothing* here was certain. It hardly seemed possible that less than a year ago his daily cycle had been so smoothly directed by the gonging of class bells and had been closed with the soothingly parental "Good night" at the end of the 11:00 news.

Of course, his life hadn't always been like that. In his early twenties—before he met Madeline—there was what he called "the chaotic years." That was when he was trying to be a painter. He tried a lot of other things too. Sometimes whole days would crumble and get lost in the effort. He lived here and there in lower Manhattan, and the only taboo he considered holy was not crossing back over to New Jersey where he had relatives—that was east of Endsville, man, that was Wombsville!

He finally blew all circuits and spent a weekend—or was it longer? —in Bellevue Hospital. When he came out and added up the charges, he realized that he was broke, divorced, and a father. The paintings he could dispose of, but Rachel remained with her mother as a reminder. It would, he realized then, take some doing to put the pieces together. It wasn't all easy. As Madeline often said when he tried to teach her the importance of schedules and planning, there's nothing worse than a reformed artist.

The microbus seemed to float over the ravine on that little stone bridge and they were right in the middle of the sunlight. It *wasn't* an April Fool's trick. It was direct sunlight, the kind that filters through trees and dapples the grasses underneath, the kind that gleams through apple blossom petals from above, making each one the source of its own shimmering glow.

"It's summer. It's summer," Trixie said from the way-back. Normally, she would have shouted it; but there was something so unreal about the transformation that even she at four could sense it. Her voice was a stage whisper—the sort one might use to express wonder and delight at say, a rose window in a cathedral. "Why didn't we come *here* to live?"

They didn't answer, preferring to believe that this particular spot had been glowing magically even in the worst of January and February when they were forced to study, eat, and play within a six-foot circle around the diesel-smelling kerosene heater.

It was the season, here, for blossoming. Scattered among the trees were bursts of white and pink which, as they passed, very slowly now, evoked from them all cries of "Ooooh" and "Look at that!" like country folk at a fireworks display.

"Here," Rachel suddenly said right in his ear. "Let's stop here." There was a kind of urgency in her voice which surprised him, but he was too caught up with the magic of the sunlight splashed on branches and blossoms to give much thought to anything.

"Yes," Madeline said. "Right here." He was already coming to a stop. There was something about this particular spot which seemed to demand it. It was both familiar and totally unexpected. He had never for a moment thought that they would find a place like this.

He parked in the tall grass by the road. They were not quite at the bottom of a truly green trough between layers of wooded hills on either side. Across the road from them the land fell away sharply down to the little river and then rose again. Some peoples at some distant time in history had terraced that hillside and planted it with trees. Tall grasses and shrubbery grew along with the untended trees, and the entire hillside shimmered in direct sunlight the intensity of which they had almost forgotten. The regular terracing somehow distorted the perspective in the manner of a medieval landscape. It would not have been surprising to see hooded hunters with crossbows or even a white unicorn grazing there. "Can we go down to the river?" Flick was asking. "Can we, Daddy?"

"Let's all go," Madeline said. There was an enthusiasm in her voice which he hadn't heard all that winter.

"You go," Ernie said. "I just want to soak up this sun." What he didn't say was that he wanted to get rid of them. The horror of togetherness was still upon him and he wanted to lie there in the grass completely freed from the responsibility of arbitrating, disciplining, encouraging, discouraging, training, or even talking with them.

"Coward," Madeline said. There was no telling just how serious she was.

So they went off, Madeline in the lead picking her way along a kind of shepherd's trail that led down to the stream, Rachel close behind her, then the two little girls scampering in a zigzag course, and finally that miserable dog, trotting with her tongue out as if it were August already.

When they had disappeared he went to the car and got the large, rattan-wrapped bottle of retsina and a plastic cup. He wondered if he had been planning this all along. He hadn't taken wine with lunch since the chaotic years, and he disapproved of Madeline's daytime drinking; but here and now a number of rules seemed to be slipping by like summer clouds.

He took the bottle and the cup across the paved road to the slope near the trail and lay down in the tall, new grass. From below came the indistinct sounds of his family descending—occasional shouts of laughter or surprise mingled with the hissing of water, katydids, and soft wind through grass.

He sipped the wine, savoring the strong pine-pitch flavor and letting the alcohol radiate within him. The bitter taste was also mellow—as odd a blend as the heat of the sun coming to him through the cool spring air. He smiled, pleased at seeing the same sort of inconsistencies within him as those around him. Somehow it put him in tune. Squinting, he let the branches of the trees above him turn into veins against the background of alternating white and blue. He was, in some extraordinary sense, looking at his own corporeal self.

It was then that he realized, between sips, that for the length of that long winter he had been blind to color. True, he had seen a lot of frescoes in these small churches. They all had traces of their original color. But during the civil war most of the buildings had been abandoned with only a vigil light or two remaining to guard them, and the brutality of time and weather had left only hints of what once must have been vivid and exciting. He was slowly learning to be clever with the camera, measuring exact distances and determining time exposures with an accuracy that he would have found tedious a decade ago. And on alternate days with perfect regularity he would write up his finds, speculating on the range of tones which neither the eye nor the camera could catch. Still, it was all speculation. When he used such easy words as "red," "blue," or "gold" in his descriptions, it was only because he wished they still existed. Those cold, dank walls had all faded. There was no way his thesis could revive them.

Thesis. The word chilled him like a temporary return of the winter's overcast. It shouldn't, of course. It was job to be done. He had been assured that it had been well conceived and that with the photographs there was a possibility of publication as well. He had learned, over the past decade, how to work steadily and efficiently. He could pull together a thesis the way he pulled together his family—fighting Rachel's mother for custody rights and at the same time struggling to develop the maturity of his child bride. No, it hadn't been easy. But he had got the thing hammered together somehow—an ungainly but seaworthy ark which was not such a bad job for one who didn't learn how to swing a hammer until late. He had played with color as a prodigal son, but now that he was his own father he had no time for games. He had to face the cold fact that his dissertation had nothing to do with art and a great deal to do with staying afloat. As a failed artist, he'd be damned if he'd end up a failed teacher as well.

He finished his second—or was it third?—cup of wine and lay back, passively letting his eyes examine the grasses next to his head. In a single long spear of grass he counted four different shades of green and yellow. Vaguely, sloppily, and with pleasure he tried to recall the tubes of paints by name—Yellow Ochre, Thalo Green, Cadmium Yellow, Green Earth. He mixed them variously. The traces of retsina, still wet about his mouth, smelled something like turpentine and he smiled. Up in the glowing fruit tree above him the white blossoms were tinged with red from the sunlight and, where shadowed, with Ultramarine Dark.

It was too much—all this color rushing back to him. He felt like a diver rising too quickly from unlit depths. In defense he closed his eyes. But even there the sun glowed through his lids—an Alizarin Crimson with a touch of Burnt Sienna. Extraordinary, he thought, that for the length of that long winter—or was it winters?—the inside of his lids showed only gray.

He may have slept, but it couldn't have been long before he heard the sound of splashing water and footsteps on the path coming up. He felt a wave of pettish resentment. They gave him so few moments by himself. The great weight was on him again. It was hardly fair.

He squinted past a thyme bush to where they would be coming out. But it was not Madeline. It was a stranger—a hooded old man. He seemed to be floating up along the path, dark and ominous.

Ernie sat up with a jolt and saw that the man was on a brown pony—a young, beautiful creature, though a bit underfed and a litle nervous. Behind the rider was a haughty black goat with a long neck. She was being led by an old, knotted thong. Occasionally she would balk, eating from this branch or that bush, but then the cord would come up taut and she would take a few quick steps to catch up.

Behind the black goat followed two little dirty white lambs, bleating protests but still following without being tethered. Ernie had seen goats leading a flock of sheep, but he had never seen lambs taught to follow so young.

Then, with sudden alarm, he saw that the final member of this troop was Skili. He jumped to his feet as if burned by an electrical charge. The pony turned and looked him right in the eye as she approached, tossing her head as if signaling; and the black goat gave a short, low cry.

He opened his mouth to shout out "Madeline! Rachel!" but the absurdity of it all was too great, so what came out was "Skili! Skili!" The dog paid no attention whatever. Ernie almost called out again when he realized that he was shouting "Dog!" in Greek and he was suddenly frightened of what the old man might do. It was a shocking insult in this land, and Ernie had no way to explain.

They were passing now, the pony struggling up the last steep part of the bank and turning where the trail ran parallel with the river. They were within fifteen feet of Ernie. The old hooded figure paid no attention to him either, keeping his mind on the trail directly in front of him. His dark face was almost completely hidden in shadows under his filthy black cowl. Even his hands on the reins were gray. Perhaps, Ernie thought, the old fool was deaf or blind. But that wouldn't account for his own sense of alarm; the old man was unmistakably evil—a cousin of Death.

Now they were leaving. The pony took one last look; the goat, close behind, gave a final bleat; the lambs and the dog trotted along, innocent and unaware.

Ernie stood there unsteadily with his hands pressed against his temples. The sound of hoofs along the trail died away. He was utterly alone, cut off both from time and from logic. He could not remember what country this was or what season it was. And then in a mad daydream he could see himself telling a squad of foreign police, "All I did was to send my wife and children down into this little glade near a river and an old man came along and. . . ."

With a sudden spurt of energy he ran along the trail in the direction the old man had taken them. It was well below the paved road and badly overgrown. He plunged forward running hard, ignoring the branches that slapped his face. How in hell had a pony got through here? But there was no route off to either side. He *had* to find them again.

Finally he heard barking and in a sudden flurry there was Skili running back to meet him with little yelps of delight. Her black and white markings flashed in the dappled sunlight. Ernie swept the dog up into his arms and rubbed her head against his cheek. And, yes, there was Flick in her orange plaid dress and Trixie in blue with an aqua sweater tied around her neck. Then Rachel: her dark hair actually iridescent as she ran toward him, face flushed with a smile. Just behind came Madeline looking proud and scared as he had once seen her after a dangerously rough day of sailing in Maine.

"Where have you been?" he was asking at the same time as the little girls were saying with delighted excitement, "We got lost! We got lost! Mummy didn't know where we were. We've been up and down the hill. There's no one anywhere to ask."

He looked at Madeline, ablaze in a sunrise scarlet sweater. Her smile hovered on the edge of tears.

"How on earth did you find us?" she said.

"We thought you wouldn't even look for us," Rachel said; and clumsily he tried to embrace them both while the little girls gamboled about and the dog yapped and wet on his foot and everyone was laughing.

"You found us, you found us," Flick chanted, speaking for them all.

"I found you," he repeated, nodding in wonder. "I found you."

I Remember the Day God Died
Like It Was Yesterday

I remember the day God died like it was yesterday. That was some time ago, of course. I've been to a number of funerals since then, I can tell you, but there's something about that one that stands out. I don't mean the service exactly. More like it was the entire day.

It was early April. I remember because I was plowing. You may not know this, but I thought of myself as a farmer then. Not much of a farm, really. A cow and a horse and maybe four to five acres being worked and hens all over the place—we never thought of keeping them inside and keyed up with lights on all night the way they do nowadays. Just scratch around, they did, and once a day Nell would throw out potato peelings and bread that'd gone bad and maybe a little corn and they'd come running, thankful for what little they could find. They got along all right, but the whole thing wasn't what you'd call a thriving farm. I'd started working part-time here at the store and I suppose there was a part of me that knew I'd end up owning it. These days there's those that make a real business out of farming and those that move into town, and there's no way to turn the clock back.

Well, as I said, I was plowing. With a horse. You don't see that much now. I always talked about getting a tractor—Ford was just beginning to make 'em—but a horse did well enough with that sort of acreage. It was one of those spring days that starts with an ice-skim on the rain barrel and by eleven has you in a sweat. I don't remember the time exactly, but I know I was sweating so it must have been late in the forenoon. And then the church bells started that tolling.

Well, I reined up and just stood there, leaning on the handles of the plow. Funny . . . I can remember the feel of the handles, smoothed with maybe eighty years' use—it had been my father's. And hearing those bells, slower and more spaced out than on Sunday, and keeping it up like it was the end of the world. It was enough to send a ripple down your back.

But of course it wasn't the end of the world. I guess we all knew that. Just the day before I was talking about it with old Jeremiah Bates at the store—he owned it in those days, but there's not many around today who'd remember him.

"From what I hear," he said in a mournful tone, "things look real bad. Couldn't be much worse." He looked as if he was about to lose kith or kin.

"I guess they do," I said.

"And there's not a thing the likes of us can do about it." I thought for a minute he was going to cry. At his age!

"Well," I said, sort of cautious, "no matter what, there'll be the plowing to do."

"That's no way to talk with Him not even gone yet."

"Maybe not," I said.

And maybe I did speak out of line because when those bells started I knew that I couldn't go on plowing that morning. No law or anything. Just a feeling of what's right. So I unhitched the plow and started leading Nell back—named her for my wife, you see. Sort of a family joke, though I can't say I ever got her to laugh over it. And all the time this tolling kept on, real solemn. There's three different churches within earshot of my place. On a stormy Sunday or during the winter when you're packed inside and trying to keep from treading on children, cats and dogs, you can't hear a one of them. But on a day like that April one, when there's just a light easterly, hell, you can even hear the deacon's rooster like he was one of your own. And the church bells themselves—why all three of them could be in the pines next the corn field.

So even in the barn currying Nell, as soon as I let up with the brush I could hear that mournful sound. Then I'd bear down again almost like I'd rather hear the swish of the brush.

It must have been a half hour before I was headed up to the house—not like driving a tractor into a barn and flicking the switch, I can tell you. Well about that time I saw my boys—they were eight and six that spring—streaking across the corn field and heading for the house. They'd taken the short cut through the woods from school and if they'd been let out when the bells started they must have made it in half the usual time, just like it was the beginning of vacation.

I hadn't really thought until then how Nell and the boys might be taking it. But I should have known it wouldn't really hit the young ones. I mean, things like that don't get through to children the way they do to adults. For instance I remember when my older brother died—it was a jolt to us all because he hadn't lived a full life. He was still in his thirties then and hadn't even married and it was just a cut from a rusty saw that did it so we were all left a bit uneasy. You know how it is—you think you can depend on forty or fifty years of living to work things through to some sort of wrap-up and then you find that chance has a good deal to do with it. So we were all a bit shaken and I think Nell even cried a bit in spite of having said only a week before that he'd never come to anything if he didn't find a woman and start in raising a family. She had a point there, though I must say that when it came to felling trees and clearing land and draining bogs—rough work like that—he taught me all I know. It came to him natural and he was happy to teach me just for the pleasure of it. But what I started to say was that my two boys, who really thought the world of him, were no more touched by his death than if he had moved upstate and we were giving him a sendoff. Oh, they were respectful enough and sat through the service without my having to scold them more than once or twice, and maybe they were a bit saddened; but I had the feeling that they were solemn more for seeing their betters solemn rather than from any true understanding.

Well, as soon as I stepped into that kitchen I knew I didn't have to worry any as to how Nell was taking it. She had her new plug-in iron going and was fixing the boys' church clothes just like it was Sunday. And the boys themselves were almost being helpful—perhaps the sound of the tolling had reached them too. The older one, Sol, sort of took over his brother as if he were the father at all of eight. "Hush up," he'd say, real serious, "and hold still while I brush your hair." It was a wonder to hear.

"I was about to call," Nell said to me without looking up from her ironing. We'd been married almost ten years then, and I'd come to know that when she talks without looking up from what she's doing, she's a bit put out. "I figured you must have heard the bells," she said. "You're too young to be hard of hearing."

But as my father used to say, there's times when the best answer is no answer, so I started washing up at the soapstone sink without a word, sloshing the water from the brass spigot. They'd brought in electricity just the year before and it still gave me a jolt of pleasure to have water just pour out on command. Simple as flicking the electric switch and filling your house with light. You can smile, but those seemed like miracles to us in those days.

"When's the service?" I asked.

"In less than an hour," she said.

I asked how she knew for sure, and it turned out that the womenfolk of the town had got things all set. There was to be a memorial service just an hour and a half after the bells started ringing.

I remember drying my face on the roller-towel next the range and telling myself to keep my mouth shut—Times of trouble are times of silence, my father always used to tell me. But I just couldn't do it.

"You mean you were planning," I said, "with Him not even gone yet? Is that what you've been doing up to church?"

"Nothing disrespectful in that," she said. "Have to plan on eventualities. And the Deacon was assisting."

"The Deacon?" I says. "Is that a fact?"

Maybe I should mention that in those days when the deacon "assisted," whatever you were doing was *right*. I mean if someone wanted to put a saloon in the vestry and got the deacon to approve, the town would go along with it. I'm not saying he *would*, of course; and I'm not suggesting that if he did, the townsfolk would *like* it; all I'm saying is that towns like ours never were the blocks of granite some people on the outside took them to be. If the Deacon said it's right to plan out a memorial service down to the last flower while at the same time praying it wouldn't be necessary, why the town would go along. And I guess it did.

We drove into town in the Franklin. That was my first car and I can remember the feel of power driving roughshod over that hill by Jeremiah Bates' place without having to stop halfway like we did with horses. Of course a new Franklin was more than a man like me could afford in those days, but I got mine secondhand from old Richards, the editor. And I can tall you that it was about the smartest investment I ever made. It got us just about anywhere we wanted to go. I used to take it to market once a week, and it got Nell down to the store in half the time it took my parents. With the self-starter she could take it alone. Gave her a bit of freedom her mother never had. There were those who thought it odd to see a woman driving, but times change and it wasn't long before the others were doing it too. Hard to imagine when you look around the parking lot today that at one time it took some courage for a woman to strike out on her own and drive that thing all by herself.

So with the boys dressed in their best blue pants and their only jackets and the Franklin jogging along and me swerving now and then to miss the mud holes that were beginning to open up—the frost was just recently out—and all of us pleased enough to be taken off our chores with a free conscience, it was almost like a spring Sunday. Actually it was a Wednesday, as I remember it, but it had all the feeling of the Lord's Day. And in a sense it was.

Now I'm not going to bore you with the service itself. It wasn't too different from what we normally have, except that the number of people there and the flowers they'd fixed up made it seem special. We had the usual prayers and the hymn singing which I guess wouldn't seem like much to an outsider but they mean a lot to one who's always heard them. Familiarity, my dad used to tell me, is like a father's helping hand. Well, there's something to that. The way young people move about today—house to house and state to state— I should think they'd feel like orphans. But maybe they've learned to live with it. Anyway, there was a lot of the old familiar hymns which wouldn't mean much to you but we'd heard them since we were little ones. And one of them took on sort of a new meaning. It was written for evening services. It starts off real slow with "Now the day is over; night is drawing nigh." As you can see, when you sing something like that in a memorial service, it turns your thoughts to death. You know, linking *day* with *life* and *night* to *death*. I mean, that's the way your mind runs at times like that. So it sort of caught me at the time. And of course there were those who felt a little teary and you could hear some nose-blowing.

And then there was the eulogy from the deacon. His voice was in good form and we were moved and even the boys could catch the tone of it and behaved themselves. In fact, Sol even was sniffing a little. I just kind of accidentally lay my hand on his to steady him a bit.

As I recall, the theme was how He had been like a brother and a father to us all . . . a brother because He'd been inside us—a companion, like—and fatherly in guiding us and punishing when there was need of it. Something like that. And then he went on to how we should always remember Him and how we owed it to Him to carry on with our chores just like He was still among us. Well, I never put too much stock in the deacon—he was just a man like the rest of us—but I think he struck the right note there. As I told him on the way out, "You give words to what we've been thinking."

I guess that's what he wanted to do because he thanked me with a warmer smile than I usually got from him and then he urged me to stick by for the church lunch.

"Church lunch!" I says. "When did you have time for that?"

"We've had things planned," says he. "The womenfolk and me."

Then he chuckles like a man who's played an April Fool's trick.

Well, that was some trick. I don't mean that a church lunch in itself was out of the ordinary. You see, in those days there were still a lot who came to church by wagon or buggy and after a four-hour service it was natural to have a church lunch there or you'd starve before you got home again. Besides, when *I* was a boy there was still another service in the late afternoon. We made quite a day of it! The idea of the church lunch lingered even after the second service was given up. People are slow to change.

But I'd never heard of a church lunch on a Wednesday. Or on short notice either. I mean, usually they start planning those things three days in advance. So apparently the deacon had worked out who was to bring this and that long before He left us. That did startle me a bit, but I suppose a deacon has to be practical just like the rest of us. I remember that when my brother was lingering with the poison working through his system and the doctor shaking his head and saying there wasn't nothing he or any of us could do—he looked a bit like the deacon when he frowned—I quietly arranged for a neighbor to take over with the milking and the feeding in case I had to go to town to plan the funeral and all. Now I'll admit that didn't make me feel too good because I'd spent a lot of time with my brother when we were young and I don't suppose we ever lied to each other when it came to serious matters. Jokes, yes; but not about living and dying. And it was clear I couldn't say to him, "Well, I've got things fairly well planned for you when you do finally let go," and to look at him and not be able to say something was the next thing to lying. So I felt badly about it and I made a point of not mentioning it to Nell—though I know now that she would have seen it in a practical way.

Anyway, the church lunch turned out to be one of the best in years. And it was about the last too. I mean, there are special occasions even now—chicken dinners to raise money for a TV set for our new minister or record player for the teen club—but the regular church lunch is gone with the horse and buggy. No need for it really. Those of us that still come to service like to get home afterwards for Sunday dinner with all the fixings.

But as I was saying, the lunch that particular Wednesday was one of the best. They had dispensed with the usual beans and frankfurters and the deacon had contributed a spring calf—mighty unusual that early—and we had a veal dinner with a potato salad and home-preserved corn with none of that artificial flavor of your frozen foods.

And we polished it off with cider. Lord, I can't even tell about it without saliva coming to my mouth. They don't make cider like that now. It's all those preservatives—hell, you might as well be drinking embalming fluid. But then it was the pure stuff pressed from the fruit that had been held over the winter in root cellars.

But I don't mean to imply that we weren't mindful of the occasion. It was in the church basement rather than outside—who could have told it would be such a good day?—and the deacon said grace clear and loud and longer than usual. In fact, without meaning any disrespect, it was hard to smell that veal and wait for the prayer to be over. But we did. We're a God-fearing people and we don't cut corners. Of course it's harder for the young ones. The deacon was droning on, and out of the corner of my eye I saw a little hand and arm sneak out like a snake across the table toward the plate full of round apple-muffins and I had to crack him a good one on the knuckles with the handle of my knife just like my father used to do to me. It was Sol and he gave a little yelp, but luckily everyone said "Amen" just then so he gobbled the muffin and said "sorry" to me with his mouth full. I don't think he meant to be disrespectful. He just got hungry the way boys do.

Well, that was quite a meal. A meal of meals!

But an odd thing happened on the way home that afternoon. We had lingered a bit over the cider and I have a hunch that the jug that they used for the menfolk had worked just a mite longer than the one that went to the women and the deacon, so we were in a loving mood as we wandered to the road where the cars were lined up together with the horses and the wagons and buggies. We all got in the Franklin and what with the warm weather and all she started up on the first turn. We were about a half mile down the road—it was dirt then —when I remembered my cigar. You see, the deacon didn't take kindly to smoking because The Book says something against it (though I could never find just where, chapter and verse), and my good wife was opposed because her nose told her it was a sin, so my only chance was driving along in that Franklin—and *then* only when the isinglass windows were stored away for the good weather.

So I stopped and opened up the tool box which in those days was convenient-like on the running board and got one of my cigars and was standing there in the road slowly drawing on it, turning it careful so as to get an even ash. The boys were sort of quiet—maybe they'd got the wrong cider—and looking at the pictures in an old almanac I keep in the car just for them, and Nell was just about asleep. It was a quiet time with crickets sounding like it was August already and what we call pinkwinks—peepers—singing from down in the swamp. There was choke cherry and gray birch along that dirt road, still dusty and leafless. And far down at the turn was that white church. Of course since then they've built the new store and the filling station and the welding shop across the street, but then all I could see from that spot was the church itself with its white clapboards almost shining in the sun. Now I suppose I'd seen that view—coming the other way, of course—a thousand times or more. And I've seen it since—there was no service *that* Sunday because of the rains and the spring mud, but we've been from time to time since then and we've seen deacons—ministers they call 'em now—come and go. But standing there at that particular time and looking back to just the trees and the church and no stores or signs or autos, a great sadness rose up in me. I couldn't account for it. Maybe it was the service or maybe I was turned a little soft with that cider, but all I know is that I felt the melancholy swirl around me like a heavy and sudden fog closing out the sun and all the old landmarks. Then—perhaps to cover my feelings—I coughed over my cigar smoke and Nell made her familiar comment how the pleasures of smoking were beyond her, and I gave my usual answer—how I wouldn't have her otherwise—and we smiled. She has a warming smile. It can cut right through a black mood. I don't know if it was that or something about the day, but I said right out of the blue: "You know, I'm going to find some other name for that horse of mine."

"I'd have no objection," she said, real pleased; and then we headed home as if nothing had happened.

And in a way, nothing had. There were still the chores to tend to. You can put 'em off, my father used to say, But you can't put 'em out, by which he meant you can't put them out of your life. And there's nothing like a middling farm to teach you the truth of that . . . though come to think of it, running a store is much the same. There's just so much that has to get done, and it's there awaitin' for you when you come back from anywhere. And so I was back plowing that same field late that very afternoon. There's worse things than plowing with a horse you know well with your hands on handles worn smooth with the callouses of your own father, and a field you've cleared by hand with your brother and crisscrossed a thousand times. I know I've cursed that field more than I can count. Every spring the frost would work up new rocks for us to pry out—Satan's winter work, my father called 'em—and there's nothing but backache in all that. And you know right well that I didn't stay there on the land as soon as there was a chance to feed my family doing something else. All I'm saying is that there were times—and that was one of them—when plowing a field was better than a lot of other things I could have been doing. You see, I was just beginning to work out of that peculiar mood I'd felt up there on the main road.

And it could be that Nell felt just a bit of it too, because I could see from where I was that she had every rug in the house out on the clothes lines and was knocking the winter dirt out of 'em. That's something I usually give her a hand with.

Later when she called me to supper I yelled back that I'd better use the rest of the sun, for her and the boys to go ahead. I guess she understood because she not only nodded but give a little wave too, which is unusual for her.

The quiet and solitude were good for a time, but after they had finished the meal Sol came down and I must say I was glad to see him. We never talked much, him and me, but we worked together a lot and that's a language in itself.

He just walked along beside me for a spell without a word and then he took over the reins, leaving the plow handles to me just as I had taught him. It's a lot easier that way, particularly at the end of a furrow where it's all you can do to get the plow turned and miss the rocks and roots without having to fuss with the reins as well. But what I remember was not so much the relief over having the job made easier—I could have ordered him down there if I'd felt the need of it—but just having him along at that particular time. The sun was low and as we turned on the easterly course with the sun behind us our shadows reached out before us. It was an odd sight, the two of us outlined against the dirt there. I suppose it was because he was a few steps ahead, but his was the longer shadow. I remember thinking to myself, "There's the man in him." And I suppose in a way of speaking that other shadow was the boy in me. I've thought of that a number of times now that he's grown up, half a head taller than me and with two boys of his own. At any rate, it gave me a good feeling to have that other shadow flickering along beside me.

Well, we finished that field by using the last scrap of daylight, and by the time we were through bedding the horse down it was dark. We started up for the house in silence, following the path more by the familiarity of it than by sight. Then all of a sudden Sol said, "It won't ever be the same, will it?"

It took me by surprise because it was the first time he had said a thing about the funeral. I didn't know it had touched him a bit.

"I don't suppose," I said, cautious like. "But there's still the plowing and seeding to do. And there'll be the weeding and the harvests. And there's nothing to keep us from going to church just like before. But it won't be the same. No."

Crossings

What do you do with a young daughter who has just gone over to Roman Catholicism? Me at thirty-six and her at ten—that's quite a span. And me an atheist. There's another span.

I'm sitting on the edge of her bed with a copy of H. G. Wells' *Outline of History* in my hand, feeling rather pious because of my attention to parental duty at the end of a very tiring and monotonous day spent revising plans for a new school in Bronxville, and she asks me straight out if it will be all right to dispense with our reading that night so she can say her prayers. It is, of course, news to me that she knows what a prayer is.

For just a moment we look at each other, mutually startled but playing it very cool, and we listen to the hiss of snow against the apartment window and it seems as if there is a hush over all Manhattan.

Now, I'm not the shouting kind of atheist. I don't write pamphlets called "The Bible Exposed" or alarmist articles about the power of Rome and I don't picket against school prayers or anything like that. I really don't feel much stronger about my nonbelief than most of my friends do about their beliefs. I never proselytize, and I've always sent my daughter to Unitarian Sunday school to keep her from feeling different.

I suppose I could be accused of being a backsliding atheist. I'm a far cry from my father. Now, *there* was a man of dynamic nonfaith.

People sometimes ask me what it was like to be brought up an atheist, and I have to stop and think. As in good religious homes, the faith of the family was so intermeshed with daily life that we could hardly separate the two. Take, for example, the grace my father said before every meal. He had a black beard like a Greek Orthodox priest, and a very low, rumbling voice that comes to me with great clarity when I recall his recitation: "We take this food remembering those who are less fortunate, humble before fate, yet proud of our labor." It never consciously occurred to me that perhaps other fathers said it differently.

On a less subtle level there were the Wednesday evenings of instruction—resurrection explained, Genesis compared with Ovid's account, Abraham set against *The Golden Bough*, and all that. But as with most religions, what stays with you is not the direct teaching but the ritual, and particularly the familiarity of feast days. Like Easter Sunday. We all looked forward to that. My younger sister and older brother and I would hurry through breakfast and then present ourselves for inspection. Our clothes had to be neither too dressy nor too sloppy. We would be sent back if we wore party shoes "like a damned Lutheran," but we couldn't look as if we were begging, either.

Then, inspection passed, we children would head for Manhattan. Since we lived on Staten Island, the trip was made via trolley, ferry and subway, in that order. The selection of exactly which corner on Fifth Avenue to station ourselves was up to us, and sometimes we would argue a good deal about this, since we all were well trained in debate. But once we had settled on a spot (sometimes by a two-thirds vote), we were rigidly bound by ritual. My brother timed us, my sister recorded, and I called out the finds. For every silk hat we spotted in the next sixty minutes we later would receive twenty-five cents. These, you see, were the Christian hypocrites off to worship a prophet who himself wore rags and preached against pomp. The fact that our totals—recorded on the pantry wall beside our annual heights— declined each year like the population of whooping cranes was convincing proof that the number of Christians was declining and that social progress was indeed a demonstrable fact. But I must admit that for somewhat less than altruistic reasons, there was a sinful portion of us that secretly hoped for a dramatic religious revival.

Exciting as Easter was, the high point of the year was Christmas. Like our Lutheran neighbors, we counted the days of December. Our own celebration, however, came on the twenty-fourth. Again there was a ferry ride to Manhattan, with all the excitement and wonder that one can experience at that age; but this time the destination was F.A.O. Schwarz. We had been given just a half-hour to cover that entire store and find the three most expensive toys on exhibit. We moved rapidly up and down the aisles, solemn-faced and tense, muttering, "You take that counter," and, "Skip that kiddy stuff," and, "I'll check the trains," all the time being watched by slit-eyed clerks who could sense only that something darkly subversive was going on.

Our finds, honestly reported, netted each of us a fifty-fifty split; half the figure was deposited in our college fund and the other half went to the charity of our choice—mine, I believe, being the Perkins Institute for the Blind, at one point, and later a local cat hospital.

But none of this, I realize now, has really prepared me to deal with a daughter who wants to recite prayers right here in my presence. And mine alone—her mother is off attending a school committee meeting again.

"What prayer do you have in mind?" I ask with splendid control, picking an imaginary flake of lint from my pants leg.

"The Rosary prayer," she says to me, as if I should have known.

"And where, Susan, did you learn the Rosary prayer?" I ask.

"From Sister Theresa."

"And who is Sister Theresa?"

"At the convent." I know what she means by this because we live on Fourteenth Street and there is a small convent smack in the middle of our block. "I go with Marie," she adds. Marie is a prematurely haughty little girl whose father is with the French embassy and who lives in the new apartment building that also is on our block.

"Regularly?" I ask.

"Afternoons. After school."

"You've talked this over with your mother?"

"I didn't think she'd understand. She used to be a Congregationalist."

This exchange has been going on straight-faced, low-voiced and almost breathlessly—like two poker players who have discovered with some alarm that they have staked most of their life savings on a single hand.

"Marie's Catholic," she says pointlessly. "Also," she adds.

I stiffen.

"Being French," I say, "I suppose she was *born* a Catholic." It is my first cautious step into argument, and I realize at once it was poorly conceived. It won't do to treat the revered Marie as a victim of a congenital defect. "People tend to follow the teachings they were brought up with," I say, groping for a retreat.

"And some don't," she says, her voice trembling just a bit. "Like Uncle Hubert." She has me there, since my older brother Hubert went High Episcopalian with a vengeance. I'm only hoping that she won't also recall my sister Tilly.

"And Aunt Tilly," she adds in a consciously offhand manner. "But I won't say prayers if you don't want me to."

"Oh, I don't mind," I say, even more offhandedly. "Not at all. It's your decision. Entirely. But"—and this is absolutely my last card— "I believe for that particular prayer it's customary to have beads." I try smiling.

And then, like those naive cavalry officers on the late show who suddenly realize that they have led their forces into a hopelessly indefensible ravine and can only watch with fatalistic wonder as the redskins pour down from both sides, whooping with glee, I see my daughter's hand dart under the pillow and pull out a rosary—black, plastic and wriggling.

So the next minute my daughter and only child is no longer beside me but on her knees at the edge of the bed, beads in hand, and I hear her voice mumbling. Only certain phrases come through to me: ". . . heaven and earth . . . all things visible and invisible. . . ."

I look down at the top of her head—long hair parted neatly and falling like the lip of a gentle waterfall. Her voice is clearer than an oboe. All grace. The prayer moves on to "Our Father"—which I have heard before—and then to "Hail Mary, full of grace, the Lord is with thee. . . ." And within me there is a most graceless battle—in the white hat is the liberal who votes the reform ticket, and numbers among his friends Protestants, Catholics, Jews, two Moslems, and one Ethical Culturalist, and occasionally attends a reasonable facsimile of the church of his choice, which makes a point of accepting anyone regardless of race, creed, or conviction; and in the black hat is a surly, provincial father who is saying to himself, My God, that prayer is *really* offensive—fruit of womb indeed!

They continue to take shots at each other, these two, but my attention wanders—I have seen the show before—and I'm caught by a sense of excitement that I cannot identify. It has the touch of the illicit without being vulgar, of an escape without being lost. But these abstractions are getting me nowhere. The little, wavering sensation collapses under the weight of analysis, and I am listening to Susan again.

Such shockingly adult language—and that repetition! Yet she is high on it, and lovely in her intoxication.

Drunk with it. This is once again the beginning of something parallel. I reach for it, but the memory is already in fragments and crumbles further. A trip on a ferry. But that is no help. My life is cluttered with crossings and recrossings. Yet I try again, because it is terribly important now to share at least a glimpse of this girl's new environment. She is my daughter, after all.

I am crossing the water now, and it is between night and day. We are flying through mists, and somewhere to the right there is the first glow of a rising sun. I feel the wet of the night air and my legs swing free, not quite touching the car floor. But this makes no sense; when I was too small to touch the floor of a car, I was too young to be up at dawn.

Susan's voice ripples on, repeating the prayer bead by bead, and the words blur. I hear an older woman's voice speaking to me earnestly, and in that car again I see this person's face—round and a little puffy, but earnest and intense too. Aunt Elnora! Of course! Until now I had thought I had no clear memory of her. But now, miraculously, she has returned to me. She is sitting beside me in the car, one hand on the wood steering wheel and the other on the black leather of the seat, and she is talking about souls within souls and how each drop of mist out there over the bay has a soul that will be born and reborn until it is ready for a richer, more complex body, and how every soul will, in centuries to come, experience the lives of plants, animals, human beings, planets, universes, and on and on—an endless system like an enormous river but without a beginning or an end.

River. That's part of the memory. Not just a metaphor, either—I can really see the water glistening out there. Actually it is New York's Upper Bay, and Aunt Elnora's splendid black touring car is the first one on the ferry—so that from my height the water speeds right under the hood as if we are in some new Jules Verne adventure, our Victorian flying machine skimming over the misty waters, to the amazement of fishermen in their dories. Aunt Elnora is saying in her contralto voice, "More than fifty or eighty or two hundred lives you've led, Peter, my boy, and the memory of them flickers by you twenty times a day, but *they've* taught you to look the other way. Oh, that father of yours! How are you going to evolve if you don't recall what you've learned? Answer me that one, Peter, my boy. Oh, the blinders they've put on you! The lives you'll have to live!"

Her voice has a vibrancy, low but with enormous reserves, like an engine that can do wonders with only half its potential power. I remember once again an aging mechanic who, years later, would ask me, "Do you recall that car of your aunt's?" I would nod, and without fail he would add, "Three rows of seats it had, with the best leather this side of Italy. Well, when I first opened up that there hood and saw *sixteen* spark plugs, I said to myself, 'Holy Christ!' and I'm not one to use the Lord's name in vain."

But now it is Susan who is speaking. I am, she tells me *sotto voce* between beads, listening to the Sorrowful Mysteries; and I'm wondering what right *they*—the sisters at that church—have to inject all this into such a young girl. There are laws against alienation of affection. Kidnapping.

Abduction! That's what my father called it. And that's why we never saw Aunt Elnora again. *He* claimed that she kept me up all night talking religion—she was active in something called the Disciples of Life—and then drove me to Manhattan, leaving before dawn, for some cultists' meeting. It made a good after-dinner story, him pointing his cigar at his listener and summing it all up with, "My own sister, mind you, *abducting* my son and spiriting him to New York and *seducing* him!"

"Figuratively speaking," my mother would add, as firmly as any woman could in that house.

I suppose I heard the story about forty times during the course of my later childhood. I always assumed that, like biblical miracles, it was rooted somewhere in truth and grew with retelling just to make life more vivid and comprehensible. With the past flooding up to me as clearly as the present, I am assured that it is all true. We really are flying over the waters of the Upper Bay, skimming just above the misty surface, to the amazement of fishermen in their dories.

We are landing now, and the great touring car roars out through the rosy maze of deserted streets; then we park. We mount the steps of a towering town house and enter a huge, crowded room. The babble of strangers ruffles me, but when a bell rings there is calm. A speaker chants and the many people answer. They have become a group and I am a part of it. Speaker and group take turns, a bell rings, a chorus recites, and the cycle is repeated again.

All the words are blurred and I make no effort to sort them out. Whatever it all means is in the rhythm and in the pressure of others standing on both sides, and this is made even clearer as my right hand is guided to the left side and my left hand, crossing, reaches to the right so that each of my hands is clasped in another's. I am too short to see anything of the room, but I know that this chain of people has been made continuous, like a string of beads. We are one. As we sway, chanting, it seems as if I am even those drops of water that died against my face and are reborn, just as I am now being reborn and will die again. The dying and coming forth glitter equally, almost like dawn light flickering on ripples of the bay.

Now there are tears forming because I have finally, again, *learned to remember* what I had forgotten—and will forget again.

"Daddy, what's the matter?" She is looking up at me with alarm, thinking that she has hurt me. "What is it?"

And for a moment she is a parent, and I know that this is the tone and the expression—perhaps even the phrasing—that she will use again as a mother long after my body has been struck down and has run back into the sea.

I cannot answer her at once. I feel as if I have been wrenched out of a dream I don't want to forget. Yet I must have been listening too, because some of her phrases still turn like water wheels in my head—"blessed art thou among women," "pray for us sinners," "now and at the hour of our death." Having no beads to hold, my eyes rest on her as the phrases turn and turn. I must have been looking very serious to have startled her so.

"Sorry," I say. "I am sorry, Susan." And my words come out stronger, more emotional than I'd intended. "Is that the end of the prayer?"

"No. It goes on and on. But. . . ."

"Well, don't stop," I say. I have the guilty feeling of having accidentally tripped her. "Can't you go on?"

She shook her head. "Not tonight."

"Tomorrow, then?"

I take her hand in mine, but somehow it doesn't seem like a natural gesture. I have long, bony fingers that look better against a drafting table. My confidence as a designer of schools fails me here, and I feel wholly inadequate. I want her to understand that wherever she has been during this episode is an important part of her, that it doesn't matter whether I have been there, that she should have the courage to explore, that—

"Boy!" she says with a sudden grin. "I sure thought you'd be mad!" I stare at her in amazement as she hops into bed as if this were any other night and snuggles down in the covers, arranging her stuffed kitten on the pillow beside her. The adult in her suddenly dies and I am allowed to be parent again. I've won. I've won!

I go over to open the window, taking pleasure in the old, familiar bedtime ritual. I feel almost like skipping. Nothing has changed. Nothing. And then I tug upward at the small brass inserts that are supposed to serve as handles. Ice has frozen the window.

"Damnation," I mutter, and am surprised at this absurd choice of archaic profanity. No one today uses a word like that seriously. With a jolt it hits me that the word, and even the intonation, come directly from my father. He is long since dead, but I feel suddenly victimized by him—and invasion of privacy on his part.

And now as I strain to open the window I see an imperfect reflection of myself in the dark pane directly before my eyes. Somehow the shadow and the frost make it appear to be a bearded face—like his.

Outrage seizes me, and I pound upward with the heels of my hands against the upper molding, temper lost.

"You listen to me!" I say to her sharply over the pounding. "It doesn't matter whether I'd be mad. Not with that. It doesn't matter what your mother thinks." I go on beating at the window, furious now. "All that's *your* business. No one else's. Your private business!"

And through all this racket I am dimly aware that she has been repeating something. I stop, breathing hard, just long enough to hear her saying, "The lock—Daddy, turn the lock."

It takes a few moments before the tumblers of my mind click into proper position. Then I reach up and turn the silly little brass-plated window lock, which was inches from my nose. After that the window zips wide open with almost no effort.

I stand there without moving, waiting for her laugh. But mercifully it does not come.

"You're queer," she says with sleepy affection. In *my* childhood that word was an insult, but she uses it all the time to mean special, or even wonderful. I remember once she looked up at the stars on a crisp April evening and said, "Hey, that's queer" with a tone almost of reverence.

"*You're* queer," I say, using her language and her tone, speaking partly to her and partly to the individual snowflakes that are zigzagging in crazy patterns through the night like three billion children pouring out of school.

Teddy, Where Are You?

Of course he's my son. I'll admit it's a little silly having a snapshot like that in a silver frame, but I never could get him to Bachrach's. He's rather independent.

Oh, don't apologize. *Most* people are surprised. I don't mean just his appearance—he *is* a bit shaggy—but his being so *old*. He was a college sophomore last fall, you know. Who'd think that little me would have a boy in college?

No, he hasn't been around much. Some of my best friends have never seen him in person. Like Felicia. Of course, she knew I'd *had* a son somewhere along the line—I've never really concealed the fact— but she just never happened to be around when he was here. That's fantastic when you realize how long we've known each other. We met the year I was between marriages, and we see each other almost every week. She was absolutely astounded when she saw this snapshot. She simply gasped. And then she said, "Darling . . . " (you know that stagy way she has). "Darling," she said, "you must have conceived at *ten!*" She's delicious.

Well, I wasn't exactly ten, but I wasn't twenty either. We matured early in those days. Which is why I understand Teddy's world. People tell me, "My God, Stella, can't you get the boy shaved and scrubbed? We can't even *see* him." But that's his *world*, you know. I mean, it's like Samson—that's where he gets his *identity*. And that's *it*, I mean really *it*, these days. Identity is everything. I know a lot of parents who don't take that seriously, but they just don't listen to the kids. There's no communication. Honestly, it's a crying shame.

Like last Christmas. For some reason he decided to take his vacation with me rather than his father. Usually he visits Theo—that's his father—in the winter break so he can get a little of that Florida sun, though how the poor boy puts up with all the criticism is beyond me. The two of them have an honest, open hatred for each other. Can you imagine a father telling his own son that he won't take the boy to the club because he looks like a hairy freak? But somehow Teddy manages to endure it. He just keeps quiet. God only knows what he's thinking. It's not very healthy if you ask me, but at least Teddy's got *one* parent who's sympathetic.

Well, it did surprise me a bit when Teddy said he was coming to see *me* in the December break, because he's always said New York just isn't a winter city. That's the way he puts it. He says New York is an autumn and spring city. Teddy's really rather poetic sometimes— which is lucky, because God knows he *looks* poetic. But anyway, this year he decided he wanted to be with his mother at Christmas, which was just lovely even though it's an appallingly busy time what with the usual parties and shopping, and it's even worse now that they've put me on the damn refugee board, which *of course* has to have its annual *thing* right at the height of the season. But I'm always glad to see my Teddy, busy or not, and that's more than I can say for a lot of mothers.

When he wrote me that he was taking the *train* all the way from Chicago, my heart bled. You see, his father won't pay a cent—not even for tuition—until the boy shaves off his beard and gets a crew-cut. I know it's incredible, but stubbornness just runs in his genes, I guess. And Teddy won't let me go to court. He wants his father to live with his own moral decision. Isn't that beautiful? Well anyway, Teddy's *tremendously* conscientious with my money, and that's why he wouldn't fly.

He arrived around suppertime, exhausted and in his usual state of shaggy disrepair. He was abolutely famished. All he'd eaten since Chicago was a can of cold spaghetti. Obviously it was my job to revive him. I told him right away he needed a good drink and a decent meal and got him off to Henri's before he could protest. Thank God I'd thought to make reservations that morning, because in the Christmas season Henri really does more business than he deserves.

Now I've always been partial to Henri, bless his flighty little heart, but listen to this:

We walk in, Teddy and I, and I spot Caroline with that extraordinary Romanian—the one who's about to be deported to *Bolivia*, of all places—and we were catching up on things in the foyer when Henri glides in, puts his arm on my boy's shoulder and says, "Deliveries go out back." Honestly! That's exactly what he said.

"*Hilarious*," I say to Henri, trying to cover as best I could—though Lord knows why I should cover for that kind of hairdresser snobbery. So I introduced them formally, last name and all with the emphasis on *Mister* and stressing my *son*, and you should have seen Henri blush right up to the glue line.

Then Caroline's oily Romanian said something about their planning to meet with friends—which was a typically Slavic lie because until his trial comes up he's about as popular as a case of radiation; and besides, later on I *saw* them eating alone. But me, I'm always trying to smooth things over, so I suggested that we all have a drink together at the bar and then each go our way as couples, and they agreed.

Now I'll admit that Teddy was not at his best. But how can you blame him? I mean, what can a *philosophy* major say to some damn *Romanian* anyway? And I realized that night that Caroline can talk all she wants about raising money for Korean children, but she just can't relate with *real* kids. I mean, she'd ask him where he went to college and what he was taking and whether he had any good teachers—just like some grandmother. I didn't blame him for mumbling answers. I mean, would you? It was about on the level of "Well, *haven't* you *grown?*" Honestly!

I told her this afterward, and she asked me what *should* she have talked about, and I told her about the *live* issues, things they really think and talk about. "You should have asked him about pot," I told her. He probably would have offered her a joint—that's a smoke—right there. "Or about the Black Caucus." After all, she knew he'd been in Chicago. "Or at least you could have asked him about the war," I told her. He would have given her a blast right between the eyes. That's the way these kids are. It's not that they're impolite, it's just that they're *very* direct. Honest, you might say. Yes, very honest. To a fault, sometimes. I tried to explain all this to Caroline, but I don't think she was even listening. She's one of those *terribly* well-meaning people who just never learn.

Well, I imagine Teddy and I made an interesting sight. I had on my white sheath—the Bergdorf thing with the high collar—and the spiky earrings Paxton had made for me in Mexico, and he had on the corduroy jacket he had slept in on the trip and no tie and of course that *incredible* hair and the beard. To me he's a big, frowzy bear who deep down is *terribly* vulnerable. Now I'll admit I did think of asking him to comb the snarls out of his beard just a bit—after all, I do have the instincts of a mother. But I kept my mouth shut. I mean, what right do I have? He's an adult. As they say, he has his bag and I have mine.

Oh, and the beads. I forgot that. They all wear these little colored beads. Very masculine, really—once you get used to them. They certainly make more sense than being choked by a tie.

So we didn't exactly blend in. And I discovered that people at Henri's are really not very sophisticated—money, but no breeding. I don't mean that they gawked, but they *peeked* at us out of the corners of their eyes. It put me off at first. I was asking him about his grades and his apartment (which, frankly, I'm glad I never saw), and I wasn't really listening to the answers partly because he spoke so low but mostly because of all this Peeping Tom stuff. You'd think we were on our honeymoon.

But after about the second drink I realized I was just being foolish. After all, hadn't I brought him up to be independent and on his own? I've always protected him against coercion. The few times Theo writes to me nowadays is to get me to put pressure on the boy, and I'm glad I can say that I've never buckled under. "Can't you get Ted to quite these political organizations?" he'd write—as if Teddy's affiliations in Chicago would damage his father's lousy marina in Fort Lauderdale. So I'd write the boy the next day saying he had *my* approval to do whatever he damn well liked. And then his father would write about forcing Teddy to shave. He even suggested *I* cut off the tuition money, too. How's that? I just sent the letter right on to Chicago with "HA!" written at the bottom. We have a good understanding, Teddy and I.

But I'm not saying that we always see eye to eye. He has his dark streak just like his father. Theo and I used to be taken as lovers even after we'd been married two years—it was that good. But every so often something—or some*one*—would turn up and bang! we'd walk out on each other. No discussion. Just bang! It went on like that for several years, on and off. Thanks to Theo's black streak. That's what I called it. And sometimes I think I see it coming through in poor Teddy. Of course, he couldn't have been nicer at dinner and all, but you can't relax completely when you have the feeling that maybe at any moment something will go wrong and everything will fall to pieces. It's a matter of confidence. I mean, after two bad marriages you often get the feeling you're skating on thin ice, if you know what I mean.

But never mind that. By dessert—Henri has perfectly *fabulous* pastries—I was feeling marvelous and maybe it was the cognac, but anyway I suggested that we take in a few of the old spots for dancing. He gave me an odd look—not really a smile, but perhaps amused. "You're not for real," he said. I decided to take it as a compliment, though you never know for sure. I assumed that he was also vetoing the dance plan. But then he said, "Like, why not? I mean, if you want to." That's about as much enthusiasm as he can muster for such low-level concerns. So off we went, me overtipping as I always do when I'm in a good mood.

As it turned out, we only got to one place. After a couple of dances it was me that suggested that we go home. Partly it was his dancing. I guess he just hadn't learned. I tried leading him through a fox trot and a samba, but it was a painful business—him with his ankle-high combat boots. And another thing: for the first time I realized what it would be like to go into some decent midtown place with a Negro date. I don't mean that as a crack about Teddy. It's the *society* that's sick. I've never been stared at like that in my life. Granted, Teddy didn't exactly match the decor—it cost me an extra five dollars to get him into the place at all—but the looks we got were more than that. They were *obscene*.

Well, at least he could tell that *I* wasn't one of *them*. I doubt if very many of his classmates have mothers who would put up with half of what I did that night.

And I guess he must have understood that because when we got back to the apartment he offered to mix me a drink. That may not seem like much, but it was a touch of the civilized boy we thought he had become in boarding school. You wouldn't know it, but there was a time when he wore decent tweeds and a tie and stood up when a woman came in the room. I know that's old stuff, and I wouldn't dream of asking him to go back to it, but somehow, seeing this bearded, woolly creature saying, "Would you care for a drink?" well, it made tears come to my eyes.

So I had another, even though I surely didn't need one. I mentioned the fact that his father had the knack of offering a drink in a way one couldn't refuse. I couldn't tell whether he smiled or not under all that shrubbery, but there was a little familiar flourish in the way he handed me the double Scotch that gave me a jolt.

That was nothing compared with the jolt he had in store for me. "Mother," he says with great solemnity, "about that apartment in Chicago. . . ." I held my breath. I guessed that he wanted something more expensive. I would have agreed to it, of course, though no one has unlimited income—even from alimony. But that wasn't it at all.

"I guess you know I have a roommate." I nodded. "But, like I guess you haven't met her."

"Her?" I asked.

"Her."

"I'd like to meet her very much," I said. I think it was the first real lie I'd told all evening. But then, he hadn't been too honest with me either. All this time I'd thought he'd been studying.

"Well, she's in town," he told me. I suggested that she drop by the next day—I'd had enough surprises for one evening. But he said she was fairly close, and could she join us that evening. What could I say?

As far as I can see, the girl must have been standing in a phone booth waiting for him to call. It took her about four minutes to ring the apartment bell. Teddy let her in, and they stood there looking at each other for a moment, not saying a word. No kiss, no greeting; just sort of a soul-search, you might say. And then he brushed the snow off her shoulders and from the top of her head. No hat, of course. She warmed her hands on the back of his neck. They were blue. All of this time I was standing behind them in the foyer, a non-person, wondering if I should retreat until the welcoming ceremony was over.

Now I must be fair. I've had two mothers-in-law who were genuinely psychotic, so I know what it is to be misrepresented. This half-frozen little waif was not quite as grotesque as what I had been imagining for four minutes. True, she wore an old, full-length army coat that gave her a bit of the Bowery look, but she didn't have flowers in her hair or paint on her face or anything like that. Under that absurd army coat she was just another college freshman in sweater and skirt. She had the standard long hair, beautiful but oh-so-solemn eyes, and a complexion ruined by pockmarks. My first reaction was pity: even with money, she'd never be really beautiful.

Naturally I had to ask what her name was. Otherwise we'd go the whole evening saying "hey you." She said it was Paula, and I was about to ask for her last name when something told me that they might think I was groping for ethnic background or something like that, so to this day I don't know whether Paula is Smith or Kovoleski. No matter.

I took her coat—I suppose Teddy would have left her in it all evening—and as soon as I felt the weight of the sodden thing I realized that she must have been standing in the snow all evening like the litle matchstick girl. It bent the wire hanger right down and slid to the floor, so I had to heave it up again, this time onto a wooden one. It must have weighed more than she did.

All the time, of course, I was chattering away about the snow, about how heavy the coat was, how chic I thought the new military uniforms were (my second lie, I'm afraid), how well Teddy was doing in college. It was a valiant job even if I do say so. You must realize that their end of this sparkling exchange consisted of unintelligible grunts. Honestly, I could have done better with a couple of Korean refugees.

But I know enough not to be offended. It's their world, and if I have to take the full burden of conversation until they think of some Major Issue to discuss, so be it. You have to make the effort.

As we started into the living room I couldn't help hearing the sound of her boots. They were cracked leather things with pointed toes—old cavalry boots for all I know—and they were caked with half-frozen slop and salt from the street. Clearly they were soaked through because at every step she sounded as if she were marching through the Okeechobee swamp. Now I *know* I shoudn't have cared one bit, but my rug is made of thirteen natural-white lamb fleeces that Paxton—he was my second husband—brought me back from Greece; and, well, I just couldn't *bear* the thought.

"Would you like to take off your boots?" I asked her.

"All right," she said. For a moment she seemed very manageable, and I felt things might go all right. And then she plunked herself right down on the floor like some Great Dane and pulled off the filthy things. When she stood up again I could see that we hadn't made much progress. Her bare feet—no socks, mind you—were as wet and as black as the boots.

"Are you hungry?" I asked her. "How about a sandwich?" It was a last-ditch maneuver—the kitchen has a linoleum floor.

She nodded, thank God. I don't honestly know what I would have done otherwise. I mean there are limits.

So I saved the rug, but there was no way to save the rest of the evening. I'm not sure what led to what. For one thing, those dreadful feet put me off. To my mind, there's nothing very attractive about even a *clean* foot. And the way the two of them sat beside each other at the table, chairs up close, she rubbing his leg, I suppose, right there in front of me, in my kitchen.

I asked her what kind of sandwich she wanted, and she just shrugged. I mean, honestly, couldn't she have said "Do you have ham?" or "How about bologna?" But no, she just shrugged and started gnawing her thumbnail. It wasn't until then that I noticed that all her fingers were bitten down to the quick and were sooty black. That got me—those nails or what was left of them. I stood there waiting for her to find a word, and I saw this picture of her installed in my son's apartment, cooking on some rusty little hot plate, handing him food with those filthy fingers, reading the letters I'd written to him, using his toothbrush. The picture may not have been fair, but it was damn clear; art nouveau on the wall, beer cans and bottles on the floor, and instead of a bed, an old mattress on the floor. Honestly, it wasn't the morality that bothered me, it was the *filth*.

Well, it was clear that I wasn't going to get an English sentence out of her, so I did my best to gather together some bread and a jar of mayonnaise and a few tomatoes, all of which wasn't too easy because that last drink Teddy had mixed me was one I really didn't need.

Of course, it never occurred to this lovely child to offer to help. That would have been terribly "straight." So they behaved as if I were the maid, talking to each other in low tones and sometimes giggling—God knows what at. I could pick up a phrase here or there, but they must have been about bands I wasn't familiar with or people I didn't know because none of it made sense. I could have been a Puerto Rican cook trying to eavesdrop. I wanted to say to them, "Kids, I'm right here in the same room with you. I'm right *here*. Look at me. Say *something* to me for God's sake." But I held my tongue; I mean, I wasnt *that* drunk, thank heaven.

And then I cut my finger. The tomato must have been softer than I expected because the knife went right through and sliced my index finger at the joint. And would you believe it, neither of those sweet children even *noticed*. I said "damn" or something like that and sucked my finger and Teddy didn't so much as look up. You'd think she'd drugged him, and maybe she had. I mean, you never know these days.

Well, from then on it was like a dream. I was looking through the cabinets for a Band-Aid, and I heard my Teddy saying, "She'll never make it," just as if I didn't understand English. "Like, she'll freak out again," he said. "Every time."

And Paula said something like "It's only the exams. She's cool until exams. I've got her going to the clinic. I don't know, but when you're up tight like that, maybe the clinic makes sense."

I was trying to make something out of that when, right in the middle of a sentence, she reached out and took *my* drink. The one Teddy had mixed for me. Not even "please" or "may I?" She just *took* it.

When she set it down, I said very clearly, "I've *cut* my *finger*," which at least made them look at me. "I can't find an antiseptic." And while they were mulling that over I grabbed my drink back again and put my bleeding finger in it. Of course, it was just common sense to sterilize the cut, but maybe I was also making sure she wouldn't go on stealing my drink. I'll admit I wasn't crystal-clear rational at that point. So for a moment the three of us watched the blood spread out in the Scotch.

"Did the knife reach the bone?" she asked me.

"If it had," I told her sweetly, "I would have mentioned it."

"Our cat has a runny eye," she said.

"Teddy never told me he had a cat," I said.

Teddy cleared his voice like an orator and said, "We have a cat." There was a little pause and then he said, "I've always wanted a cat. So Paula found this one. In a used-car lot. But, like pus comes out of its eye."

"Get it to a doctor," I said.

"Doctors don't see cats," Teddy said.

"There are cat doctors," I said.

He opened his eyes very wide. "Crazy!" he said.

"Oh no!" I said. "I mean *human* doctors who see *cats.* You know. Vets."

"Not in our neighborhood," he said.

"Of *course* there are, I said.

"In out neighborhood they *eat* cats."

I gasped and turned to Paula. If she had smiled it would have been a joke, but she was solemn as ever. She even nodded. "It started with the Haitian family down the hall," she said, "but then some of our friends ——"

"*Enough,*" I said. I didn't want to hear another word about eating cats or runny eyes or about Paula. It just seemed impossible to me that my Teddy had gotten himself into all this. He had *never* liked cats. I'm sure of it. I mean, if he had said anything at all about wanting a cat, we would have got him one. A healthy one. We never deprived him. It was as if somehow I didn't know him at all. My own son. In all his childhood he never even *mentioned* cats.

I suddenly felt very, very tired, and closed my eyes for a moment. And when I opened them I saw that this incredible girl had snatched up the half-made sandwich and was wolfing it down. The way she ate, it sounded the way she did walking in those wet boots.

"You seem very hungry," I said, holding on to the edge of the table, my other hand still submerged in my drink.

"Two days on this cold spaghetti," Teddy said. "That's a real down-trip. Two days on the road."

"Road?"

"Hitchhiking."

"You said you took the train."

"I said we *might.* That was to keep you from psyching out."

"But I sent you money."

She was quiet during this exchange—except for the slurping sound of her devouring the tomatoes one after another. I hadn't noticed it before, but she had unpleasantly sensual lips for one so young. I guess I was staring at her when she looked up, half a tomato still in her mouth, and said, "The money—it wasn't really ours."

"Of course not," I said. "But it was *his*."

"We share," he said. "Everything." He let the word hang there. I understood—for the first time, I guess—that from then on whatever I gave to Teddy, anything at all, would be shared by this girl. I felt dizzy—loss of blood maybe—and sat down. I took my finger out of the glass. It had stopped bleeding, but the skin had puckered. I stared at the cut line wondering if it would leave a scar. I have a thing about disfigurement. For some reason it all seemed her fault.

"What on earth did you come here for?" I asked her suddenly. "I mean, Teddy's free to lead his own life, but. . . ." It was hard to find words. I turned to him. "Why did you have to bring her back here? It's just plain mean ———"

"He's not mean," she said quickly. "Stella, believe me, we worked this out together." So now it was going to be Stella and Paula, woman to woman. I braced myself. "You've been sending this money," she said. "It's what we live on. Like, it's no good if we don't level with you. So here I am."

"That's the way it is," Teddy said.

There was something touching about that, I have to admit it. They got to me. Almost. I tried to pretend that she was one of the family already. I really tried.

"I suppose you help out with some kind of part-time work?" I said. I smiled, until she shook her head.

"Why not?"

"Why should I? I to to classes. I mean, we get along on what Teddy gets."

"You don't even *try* to get a job?"

Teddy threw up his hands. "Holy, holy, holy! What's so holy about work? Have *you* ever worked? We get along on what we get. Like you. Where's the super-sin in that?"

"I'm not talking about sin," I told them. "I'm not a *moralist*, for heaven's sake. But there are limits. I pay for my own son, but there's nothing in the books that says I have to pay for some coed who moves in on him." I looked her in the eye and said, "Can you give me one reason why *I* should pay for *your* living expenses?"

She looked me right back and said, very softly, "Love." And then she started biting her filthy thumbnail.

Can you imagine it? What on earth did she know about love? I mean, honestly, she was about the most unlovable creature on earth. Well, I really let them have it then.

"I don't know what on earth *you* know about love," I told them. "You've got no right to even *use* the word. But I'll tell you this. Love or no love, there's no law that says I have to support some cheapside bordello." Teddy was standing up, but he had it coming. "The rent's not all," I told him. "There's no law that makes me pay for next term's tuition." I took a long drink. "Why should I pay to let you lie in bed with some teenage prostitute?"

That was harsh. I'll admit that. In bad taste. I think I apologized, but Teddy just stared down at me wide-eyed as if I had just grown fangs.

"Wait a minute," Paula said suddenly, "do you want to see him in the army? Is that it? Or in jail?"

Well, I honestly hadn't thought of it that way. It was a jolt. But there was panic on her face. I wasn't thinking very fast, but it came to me finally that these were two places where she couldn't get at him. Maybe I smiled. I don't know. But she was saying—shouting almost, "She *does*. Oh Jesus, she *does!*"

Does what? I was wondering. What's she saying? But nothing really made sense then, and they were pushing by me to get out of the kitchen, and all I could think of saying was that no one could use profanity like that in *my* house, and there was a kind of scramble for coats at the door while I mixed myself a fresh drink with my back turned to them, waiting for an apology.

And all I heard was the click of the door. Not a "thanks" or even a "so long, Mom." Just the door closing and the two of them going out without anything decided.

I could hardly believe it. I stood there by the window for quite a time, watching. You get a long view from the fifteenth story. It was snowing heavily then, and the traffic along the avenue had almost stopped. They finally came into view and paused for a moment in the circle of white light from the streetlamp as if they didn't know where to go. Then I saw those two small forms, arms around each other, moving down the avenue to God knows where. I kept saying his name over and over like a chant, thinking that he would look up. But he didn't. The apartment suddenly seemed very cold.

Oh, I knew then that something terrible had happened. I'd been through it before though I don't know just when. But even now in the sobriety of days upon cold days, I wonder what I should have done. And what I should do now? He never re-registered. So now I don't have any idea where he is. Does he even *know* what he's done to me?

Mars Revisited

"Like I'm telling you," the sergeant said, "th' kid could be any-where. But he's not here. So if you want to keep looking, go with the patrolman over there."

Frank Badger turned to see a patrolman elbowing his way through the crowded headquarters, heading for the door, apparently in a hurry. But Frank hesitated. He wanted to ask the sergeant at the desk *why* he was supposed to follow the patrolman and what the man's name was and where he was being sent. He didn't like the idea of nodding or saluting or doffing his cap and running to do what he was told. At forty-two he'd outgrown all that.

But the sergeant had turned to argue with three men in dark suits —detectives or perhaps suspects—and already the patrolman had made it out into the street, so Frank didn't really have much choice.

He had to hurry to catch up. It wasn't easy. The room swirled with activity. He squeezed by a desk where two reporters were questioning a man in a pinstriped suit who might have been an alderman or a prisoner; he pressed himself against the wall to let a handcuffed pair go by; behind him in the next room three policemen were talking with a long-haired creature of undetermined sex. He found himself staring at everyone, a bewildered Adam trying to find names for each new object he saw. But that was nonsense. He wasn't a part of all this. It wasn't as if he'd been arrested. He hadn't even been asked to appear. He was only a father looking for his son. He was just following up a rumor that the boy was being held by the police in this city.

The uncertainty of it all had left him unsettled. He had spent three hours in a jet and was dizzy from two changes in time zone, from four shifts in altitude, from the jarring contrast between the sweet-talking stewardesses and the surly desk sergeant whose language, he recalled now after so many years, was the language of all sergeants everywhere. And now the patrolman he was to follow had disappeared through the door out into the night and he, Frank, had better get his ass out of there. . . .

The walls spread to the size of a warehouse and the blues of the uniforms faded to khaki. It was brutally hot and humid. He could smell the greasy dubbing which they had smeared over their new boots and the sweat of a thousand inductees being herded. They had been lined up by barking sergeants whose voices echoed up to the steel rafters and back, and now they were told to lay out their gear— all their belongings which had been carefully packed into duffle bags at four that same morning. And when they had spread out every last thing—every sock, belt, shirt, underpant, photo, toothbrush, condom, book, packet of letters—all of it lined up neatly on the sooty, paper-littered floor, they stood at attention for an hour for an inspection which never came.

And of course when the order was given to pack up again, they were to do it "on the double," they were to "get the lead out of their ass," they were to "look alive" as they stood alphabetically in groups of fifty for another half hour, this time "at ease," speculating to themselves and in undertones to each other where they might be going. That was all more than twenty years ago, and Frank couldn't remember what city that warehouse had been in, but he could feel with right-now clarity how the sweat ran steadily down his neck, shoulders, and back, tickling as it plowed little furrows through the film of coal dust which clung to his skin.

He was out in the street now, looking for the patrolman. A squad car was coming in with lights flashing and a number of pedestrians stood about—the same kind of crowd that gathers for accidents. The patrolman was getting into a second car parked further down the street. Frank ran and opened the back door just as the motor started.

"The Desk Sergeant said for me to go with you."

He paused as if by some reflex he was asking for permission.

"Well, get in then," the patrolman said.

"Front or back?"

"Jesus, will you hurry up?"

Since it was the back door he had opened, he got in that one, moving awkwardly and stumbling, half falling, over two civilians already sitting there.

"Sorry," he said, and immediately wished he hadn't. He would have to watch out for all those little phrases of accommodation with which the civil world oils its conversations. He would have to tighten up again.

They drove through an endless slum, an uncomfortable section in a strange city. The summer's heat had squeezed all the residents from their apartments down onto the steps and out to the sidewalks. The patrolman drove at a moderate speed and used no siren, but the red roof light was on and in response to it every face in every group revolved slowly, without expression, following the car as it passed.

The two passengers beside him paid no attention to the street scene. They were preoccupied in a silent search for cigarettes and matches. It was complicated by the fact that the left wrist of one was handcuffed to the right wrist of the other. It was impossible to tell which was the prisoner and which was the captor.

Finally the one whose right hand was free found a crumpled pack in the other's shirt pocket and a Zippo from his own and placed a bent cigarette in the mouth of the other and lit it. Frank could remember placing a cigarette in his wife's mouth some twenty years earlier when they were first living together, seizing time on furloughs and treasuring the nuances of intimacy.

He wished he had made it clear when he first got in that he hadn't been told where he was being sent. It seemed ridiculous to admit at this point that he didn't have the slightest idea where he was going or even where he was. As a civil engineer specializing in bridges and aerial expressways it was his job to deal in facts. Mystery or even uncertainty was at best unprofessional. It would never occur to him to spend a summer's afternoon exploring back roads without a destination; nor would he normally be willing to follow the orders of someone he didn't know and travel with strangers who wouldn't say where they were going.

Closing his eyes he could hear the endless "click-it-ti/click-click-it-ti/click" of that old troop train, the creak of its wooden sides, the muffled mutterings of poker players in the aisle, a harmonica somewhere, distant snoring. A night and a day and another night without the slightest idea whether they were headed southwest to Texas ("that's where they do desert-survival training—no canteens") or south to Georgia ("they make 'em swim across swamps at night") or west to the Rockies ("Arctic survival—I hear two out of ten die in basic").

At night they tried to read their directions from the stars, peering upward through the filthy windows, but there wasn't a man there who could tell north from south in that way. And by morning it was drizzling so that the sun was no help. At some point that day the train waited for an hour in a sodden wasteland of stubbled, burned-over fields and red clay. No cattle grazed here and no cars moved along the puddled dirt road. But from somewhere came a tattered delegation of black children, rain-streaked and unnaturally solemn.

Frank and all the others leaned out the windows and shouted, "Where are we? Hey kids, where are we? What state?"

But the children didn't understand and held out their hands saying, "Mon-ey? Penn-y. Gimmie penn-y."

The soldiers, mostly Northerners, were incredulous. "Je-sus," one of them said, "they've drove us clear to North Africa." They all laughed and started pitching pennies, watching the children scramble for them in the puddles. This was even funnier. Frank pulled back from the window, brooding about where these children were, where they all were, and where in hell they were going.

"Where are we going?" Frank asked abruptly.

"Never mind about that," the patrolman said.

It seemed needlessly hostile until he realized that the driver may have assumed that it was the prisoner who spoke.

"Look," Frank said, "you don't have to talk to me like I was under arrest. I'm just looking for my son and they told me to go with you. They didn't tell me where we were going."

"We can't talk with a suspect in the car. Regulations."

His tone was neither reprimanding nor friendly. It was devoid of human emotion. "Besides," he added in the same voice, "if you'd kept your boy home he wouldn't be in trouble."

Bastard, he muttered in silence. If it weren't for that uniform. . . .

He had almost forgotten what it had been like to be hemmed in by uniforms. Below him, the old sergeants, leftovers from the peacetime army, their minds addled by military life, yet still ready to discredit the young officers over them. And, worse, the deal-making colonels who knew they had to make good before some idiot stopped the war. And those earnest captains, one notch above Frank, insisting on the rights of elder sons because they had entered the war just one year earlier—the incredible subtleties of rank.

He was startled by the siren. It was not a wail but just a low growl, the sound of a large and threatening dog. The streets were almost without traffic, but they were more crowded with pedestrians; and almost as if by reaction to it the driver was going faster.

It was a mixed neighborhood and the headlights picked up white shirts against black bodies and some whitely bare chests. No one ran from the path of the car; they merely walked with insulting lack of concern until they were just barely out of range. Occasionally one would raise a fist or a finger. Frank wondered whether they viewed him personally as a friend of the police or as a prisoner. But how could they tell when he wasn't sure himself?

They paused at a cross street while four fire trucks passed by, wailing. And then patrol cars. When they started up again they turned and followed in the same general direction but not as fast. And in four blocks they had apparently arrived somewhere.

The driver parked on a side street together with an array of squad cars, patrol wagons, and a couple of ambulances. The crowd in the street, a mixture of races and ages, was scattered and calm, but the mystery of its presence—its mere existence—struck Frank as ominous. It was like the armored half-track parked under the streetlight, motionless but as arresting as if it had been an enormous armadillo. Police floodlights lit the entire area with sharp contrasts, making the scene into a moonscape.

The driver got out and opened the door for the two handcuffed civilians who emerged awkwardly. The three of them headed up the steps of a many-storied, rambling brick building which could have been an old hospital or an enormous city high school. Every window was lit.

Again he hesitated. It seemed impossible that this slum castle would have anything to do with his son, and it seemed outrageous that the driver expected him to trot along obediently like some jeep orderly. Back in the real world Frank had thirteen draftsmen and a secretary under his command and he had forgotten what it was to be treated like a recruit.

But it was clear that if he stood there much longer he would be demoted to just another onlooker. He'd get nowhere that way. So he ran, once again, to catch up.

An adolescent-looking guardsman—a boy soldier—blocked the door with a bayoneted carbine held diagonally before him. His head was too small for his helmet and his Adam's-appled neck too scrawny to fill his collar. He was the original cartoon of a hayseed recruit, the model for Sad Sack, a joke; he also held his bayoneted carbine with shocking self-assurance.

"D'you have a pass?" the boy asked.

"I'm with the patrolman."

"What patrolman?"

"The one who just came in with the suspects."

"You on the force?"

"I'm a witness. They need me in there." He tried to muscle by, but in an instantaneous, perfectly executed movement, the soldier spun his rifle to the horizontal position where, chest high, it was poised to send the intruder hurtling down the stone steps to the sidewalk below. And it was entirely clear to Frank that the soldier would do just that if he had to, not in anger or fear but in the line of duty the way a meatpacker slings a side of beef.

"Look," Frank said, trying a new approach. "I think my boy is being held there."

"I'm not allowed. . . ."

"He's about your age. I don't know what he's done, but I want to get to him. Just let me look and then I'll get out."

"We got orders," the boy said, but all self-assurance was lost.

"Could you check with someone?"

"Well, wait here a moment."

Incredibly, the boy soldier was gone and Frank walked directly into the large foyer, moving fast. He expected a heavy hand on his shoulder at any moment.

Almost at once he was in an enormous room—some kind of armory or exhibition hall—in which hundreds of people were working with intensity. The place hummed like a nest of hornets. A semblance of order had been attempted by walling off sections of floor space with Street Department barriers; desks had been improvised by laying doors across saw horses; crude signs had been scratched out in marking pen with titles such as *"Medical Aid," "Interrogation," "Surveillance,"* and *"Arraigned."* Directly in front of him was a real desk—ancient, scarred, and official. It was covered with scattered documents, typed lists of names, and empty coffee cups. The sign, written on the back of a torn placard, read *"Chief Expediter,"* and beside it was a small American flag on a lead base. The swivel chair which was behind the desk was empty.

Frank waited there, letting waves of busy people ebb and flow around him. He wanted to stop someone, anyone, and ask him what in hell was going on. It seemed incredible that all these people— police, detectives, soldiers, students, blacks and whites in the street —knew perfectly well what was happening and that he, Frank, was still in the dark. It wasn't as if he were uninformed. He read two newspapers and three periodicals of assorted political hues. He would have known if this city had ever been characterized as "racially torn" or prone to student strife. No, it was just another city and all of this had been going on behind his back. It chilled him to think that perhaps this scene was being repeated in cities all over the country.

Suddenly he wished he hadn't come. It was a slim lead anyway—just a phone call from an adenoidal young man saying that Francis was being held by the police in this city. But why on earth here? It was miles from the boy's college. And it seemed impossible that a student with such good grades could be deeply involved in anything political.

At his wife's suggestion, Frank had brought along the boy's college transcript. It would, they thought, serve as evidence of good character. Remembering this now, he was startled at how naive he had been before he stepped off that plane into all this. But how could he have known? He recalled for the first time in years a "V-mail" letter from his mother which had arrived after the three-week nightmare in the foothills of Anzio. She was an unusually well-informed and intelligent woman who followed the war day by day in the newspapers and by radio, and she showed her concern by serving on the Rationing Board without pay, yet she was capable of urging him to instruct the drivers in his unit to make greater savings in gasoline by avoiding quick starts and by coasting down hills. It seemed to him then that the wall between him and the civilians back home was more impregnable than that between him and the enemy.

It was no use waiting for the chief expediter. Perhaps he didn't really exist. So he went over to *Interrogation*, where men in civilian clothes, usually in pairs, were questioning suspects. There were ten or twelve such groups going on in the little corral. The prisoners were mostly college-aged but highly varied in appearance. From where he stood he could only see two who had the traditional long hair and beads. The others could have been pulled from the ranks of inductees—some black, some tan, and a majority white; some in torn T-shirts, some in sleeveless denim jackets, one in a rumpled suit, several in polo shirts. One had a filthy rag tied around his forehead and another held a handkerchief to a cut on the side of his neck; but the rest were uninjured.

Frank stared at this group longer than it would take to determine that his son was not among them. He began to understand, quite slowly at first, that his son *could* be among them. One of the boys looked past his interrogator at Frank and his expression was derisive. His son had given him that look from time to time. But he checked his own thoughts, remembering that the boy's name was Francis and that he hated to be called Son or, worse, Boy. Francis. He deserved to be called that. It would be a hell of a thing to act out the fantasy he had on the plane while still 60,000 feet above all this, a scene in which he walked down the long, sterile corridor of a model penitentiary to the designated cell and to greet the prisoner with, "Well, Son, how did all this come about?"

The plainclothesmen were through with that student and had him sign something and sent him over to the other side of the pen where fingerprints were taken. Frank could hear one of them say " . . . over to *Surveillance*," and as the boy started to leave the officer added, "So don't try anything funny because you can't get out of here without a pass."

This reached Frank like the "thunk" of a slide-bolt. Intuitively he looked around for windows and saw none.

"Hey," he said to the boy as he passed. "I'm looking for someone. Maybe you know him." He paused, but got no encouragement from the boy. "His name is Francis. Francis Badger."

"Like if I knew, Dad, I wouldn't tell you."

And he was gone. Frank's hand curled up into fists but there was no one to hit.

He went over to *Arraigned*, wondering if at this point he would recognize his Francis. Perhaps someone would have to introduce them as, in fact, they had to when he finally came home from Bremerhaven at the end of the war. "This is Francis," someone had said, and all the adults there laughed uneasily as the father picked up his perfectly strange son, two years old already, and held it awkwardly, the two of them solemn and uncertain.

Arraigned was a larger pen than the others, and was furnished with greater sophistication—it had benches. The prisoners lolled, half-reclining. Some dozed. They appeared to be as unconcerned as sunbathers at the beach. But as soon as Frank reached the barrier ("Road Closed, P.D.") they all turned to him as if he had orders for their disposition.

The watchdog was a first sergeant, National Guard, who must have weighed 250 pounds and flaunted his girth with a tieless khaki shirt which strained every button. His face was red, round, and sequined with beads of sweat.

"*Yes* sir," he said, Amos and Andy style, taking Frank as a plain-clothesman.

"I have a boy here who . . ."

"You're the father?"

"Yes, his name is . . ."

"How th' hell did you get in here? You can't be here. You're outside, Mac. You can't be in here."

"But I *am* here." Frank was not certain.

"You're not on the force and you're not being held, so there's no way you could get in."

A regular army major came up, talking fast. "What th' hell is this? Don't block the passageway. What's going on here?" And to Frank, "You authorized?" And to the sergeant, "Who is this guy anyhow?" He looked like a welterweight boxer who was about to take on two opponents at the same time.

"Man says he's looking for his son."

"Can't be. No relatives in here."

"That's what I told him. 'No relatives in here.' I told him that."

"I mean, we can't let just any sonofabitch in off the street."

"I told him. He can't be in here."

"Then tell him to get the hell out," the major said.

"He's got no pass. He can't leave."

"Give the sonofabitch a pass, then."

"How can I? He's unauthorized."

There was a momentary pause which was broken by a third man, a tall, angular civilian with a gray suit and a face to match. The two soldiers stepped back for him like well-behaved boys.

"You have a son who might be here," the man said, reviewing the case. "You have reason to believe he might be here?"

"Well, I just got this telephone call and. . . ."

The gray man simply led Frank into the pen and sat him down on a low stool. It was as if the door he had been pushing against had suddenly opened and sent him tumbling into something he wasn't prepared for.

"Have a cigarette," the government man said. Frank took one even though he had given them up two years earlier. The major lit it for him. The National Guardsman with the straining buttons stood there with his thumbs under his belt, exuding sweat. His stomach was twelve inches from Frank's left cheek.

"Nice kids can get mixed up with the wrong crowd," the government man said. "You see it all the time. Nice families. Nice kids. Sometimes it's drugs. You wouldn't believe some of the things we see. Then it's politics. You know, leftists, anarchists, hard-core stuff. Parents lose contact. They just don't know. They'd help if they could, but they just don't know what kind of trouble the kid is in. So that's where our job begins. We try to pick them up and set them straight."

Frank, in spite of himself, nodded. In spite of himself? Hell, it was all reasonable enough. It was what a neighbor might say. It was what *he* had said from time to time. After all, wasn't that why he was here? If the boy was in trouble, it was Frank's job to set him straight.

Yet, somehow, sitting there on the dunce's stool, walled in by various authorities, he wasn't sure. The simple alliances of the past weren't holding as they should. If the four adults here were on the same side, why was one of them on a stool looking up at the other three? And why was he scared?

"So maybe there came a time," the government man said, "when your boy went along with the crowd for kicks. And then he found himself in trouble. Real trouble." For some reason, this prompted his first smile. But it vanished almost at once and he pulled a spiral notebook from his pocket. "Your son's name, age, and address, please."

Frank paused. The three of them waited. The sounds of the armory blurred in a distant, rising wind. The unaccustomed cigarette made him dizzy, and he could feel his loyalties shift and heave under him. He was for a moment back at that mill in northern France, the windy night hissing through the charred trees and empty windows. The foot-by-foot advance through Italy had recently become a crazy rush of 60 and 100 kilometers a day and his group, demolition experts, was well beyond the advance lines defusing the explosives with which the Germans had so thoroughly mined each bridge. And somehow, almost unintentionally, his special detachment of eighteen men had ended up with five prisoners—not men but kids, end-of-the-road Nazis, not one of them eighteen yet, two still smooth-cheeked, all hungry-eyed and lice-ridden. They were a pain in the ass for a unit that was supposed to move fast. So the next morning Frank was waked with a cheerful shout, "Hey, who wants to go shoot the Krauts?" The shouter, a captain in command, had adopted the voice of the recreation director at a borscht-circuit resort.

Frank, a mere lieutenant, said, "Are you kidding? Execution? Those kids? You want me to include that in our next report?" *No, no,* that was not what he had said. He had said, "Count me out." That's exactly what he had said. Then. The other answer was the one he had said a hundred times in daydreams. But the kids were dead and not even buried. Thrown in a farmer's well. And he had said, his exact words, "Count me out."

"So what's his name?" the government man asked again. "Once we get him on the list, we'll straighten him out."

Twice in one lifetime? Frank thought. It was not courage that drove him but the horror of recriminating daydreams.

"John Doe," he said.

"No jokes now. This isn't a Micky Mouse show, you know."

"I don't know what you're talking about. My name is Doe. Jack Doe. My son is John."

The gray man's pencil stub paused over the clipboard caught between trust and fury. He looked questioningly at the other two. The sweating sergeant was given courage.

"It can't be John Doe," he said. "That's everyone. He can't be John Doe."

And in their moment of indecision, Frank sprang up and jumped over the police barrier. Running, he heard a police whistle and a shout behind him. He felt an exhilaration sweep through him, flushing two decades of bad dreams.

He ran through *Medical Aid*, stumbling over stretcher cases, and headed for the stairs which led up. They were roped off with a sign which said "No Passing," but he cleared it with a good jump. He thought he heard angry voices behind him, but he couldn't afford to look back and the air was filled with the sound of his own feet pounding against the old metal stairs. He took two or three flights and then instinctively shifted his course and headed down a corridor of offices. All the doors were shut and locked against him except for the men's room.

He had just bolted the door behind him when he heard shouting and the sound of feet in the hallway. They passed, rattling doors, and then returned. By that time Frank had the window open—filthy opaque glass—and was out on a fire escape. He closed the window behind him, surprised at his own logic. It had been years since he had experienced fear and he had forgotten that clear-headed energy which glands can produce.

Out there in the dark he was abruptly aware that he was high above the avenue. He must have climbed more flights than he had thought. Below him, police floodlights swept the streets. The crowds, more active now, moved in long ripples across the black river. Soundlessly a red fist leapt up and he could see that a car had been rolled over and set afire. Sirens came to him like winds sighing through the rubble of a gutted city. And a strange combination of smells—the iron of the railing he was gripping, oily smoke, and the faint acidity of teargas which reached him through the open spaces of time from basic training at. . . . Odd how the name had escaped him while the smell lingered.

And now from down there the sound of firecrackers, a happy celebration, kids having fun, the family gathered as a clan for Independence Day. *Crack!* and the sound snapped into focus and he dropped to his stomach, feeling naked without a carbine in his hands.

It shouldn't, he told himself, faze him. He'd spent time behind enemy lines before. He had lived through a two-or-three-day nightmare trying to get back across an unfixed line of demarcation, trying to identify his own side, avoiding fire from his own unit, clawing to get out of a dream which was contained within a dream within a dream so that hour by hour and day by day he only moved from one box to the next, never quite catching sight of reality. But that was another life, a kind of group memory for him and his generation.

No, this shouldn't faze him—except for the fact that he had spent twenty years proving, year by year, that those nightmares had never occurred, that he had never reeked with fear, had never been propositioned by death, had never fired blindly and watched shadows of himself falling, had never struck a skull with his carbine butt because the man was flipping like a fresh-caught fish and was making sounds no human could be expected to tolerate.

For two and a half decades he had commuted between a muted family and an orderly office, creating life to replace that which he had taken, designing spans for the smooth flow of traffic, willingly washing in and out from work with the tide of his generation, sweeping with daily strokes like a hand over a blackboard, erasing, erasing.

Which is the lie? he thought. Which is the lie? For a moment an imaginary part of him walked down that fire escape, untouched by that which simply could not be happening, and turned to a friendly cop, smiling, and asked where he might find a cab which would take him to the airport. Surely he was a neutral in a foreign land; surely they would respect his passport and lead him through chaos to the airlines desk, there to be treated as an adult whose credit rating gleamed golden like the eagles of a major general.

Was he out of his mind? He'd be shot, going down there, slithering down a dark fire escape like a sniper. Killed. No metaphor. Dead. Never mind the goddamned issues, he told himself. Leave that to the civies. Let the commentators wax eloquent over what builds the fighting spirit. In the now and here he was lying on his stomach on the metal grate, his brow pressed against the iron, his body unprotected.

And in instant confirmation, a spotlight dashed his eyes like spray. He could see nothing but a milk-white glare. He was on his feet at once and racing up the fire-escape flights, the light losing him and then catching him, raking him like a cat's claw.

Above him was the parapet. Along it were three or four heads like pumpkins. They urged him on, identifying themselves not with uniforms but by tone. And when he reached the top, he wondered if he had strength to climb over. But a clutter of arms seized him by the jacket, arms, shirtfront, and hauled him roughly, lovingly over the edge. He collapsed in the welcome dark and heard someone say, "Let him catch his breath. I'll stay with him here. The rest of you go two buildings over. Make noises."

Frank breathed deeply, aware that he was now back with his own detachment. The great booming, buzzing confusion of the conflict hushed. Years ago he had learned that in times of crisis, all loyalties and all logic shrunk finally to the level of the squad.

He lay back, still gasping for air. Above him, way above, he could see the green wingtip light and the blinking white taillight of an airliner. It seemed preposterous that a hundred or so people could be settling down to an evening highball, copies of *Time, Look,* and *Fortune,* soothed by the familiarity of Howard Johnson decor, Muzak, and the cooings of stewardesses. Only that morning he had been doing just that. He was reading a "literary" best seller which described in intricate detail—like an elaborate etching—the lives of bored New Englanders who had turned to sex for therapy. Flying at 60,000 feet, the work seemed at least possibly relevant and vaguely stimulating. Now it reminded him of the early Fitzgerald novels which he had skimmed with derision in the army hospital outside

Milan. No wonder he had left it in his seat.

From the corner of his eye he could see the bearded form who had elected to remain with him. He sat with his elbows on his knees, methodically chewing gum. He could have been some French resistance fighter. He could have been his son, Francis. Francis who had insisted on his full name ever since he read about the saint. Yes, this could be Saint Francis responding not to the birds but to the killers of birds. Can there, he wondered, be love without a corresponding rage?

There was no answer but the catcalls and obscenities shouted from a distant roof, delivered for Frank's protection.

"I got involved," Frank said with difficulty, still sucking in air, "looking for my son. Francis Badger."

"I know him," the bearded one said.

"Is he all right? Arrested?"

"He was. But he got out. Same way you did."

"He's up here?" It seemed impossible.

"The other side. He got down and across. He's O.K."

"How do I get up there?"

The boy didn't answer for a while. He picked up gravel from the roof and rattled it around in his hand like ideas. Then he said, "Don't go up there. It's not your thing. We'll get you back."

Frank nodded. Of course he would go back, perhaps even looking much the same. Still, it seemed terrible, that black river that flowed between himself and Francis.

"Suppose you'll be seeing him?" he asked.

"Sure. I'll tell him you were up here looking for him." Then he laughed—a kind of quick snort like a poker player who is caught off balance by a good card. "That's something," he said. "That's pretty good. I'll tell him you gave a damn."

And then they were off over the rooftops, heading back to the home front where the civilians—even his best friends—would listen carefully but with little comprehension to his account of the war.

Estuaries

Summers I take my family up to Worwich, Nova Scotia. That's a long way from anywhere. They remind me of that. It is also prone to fog and periodic drizzle. The wetness drifts in from Arctic seas. It is a fine mist like the kind we used to have on Cape Cod when I was a boy. But here the dampness is colder. It seems to reach for the marrow. They remind me of that too.

But where else can you find sea frontage these days? How many professors of history do you know who have 953 acres untouched by the corruptions of our society? I remind them of that.

I am sitting here in my study on the second floor. I am at a desk I built right in the dormer window. It was a stupid place to build a desk because it looks out on rolling pasture and then marshland where the sea fingers its way up into the Worwich River. Right now, the sea is retreating, trickling out. Very symbolic, I say to myself. The sands of time. My mind's been working like that lately.

I am forty-five and have a wife who plays excellent tennis, two boys in their teens, and a daughter named Hildy who is eleven. She is a pantheist, a mystic, and a reincarnation of an eleventh-century princess who dies young of dragon wounds.

I am forty-five and have published numerous articles on twentieth-century social history and politics. In spite of the fact that they appeared in magazines like the *Nation, New Republic,* and the *Progressive,* they won me an associate professorship for whatever that's worth. Then I wrote a book which won me a professorship and $3,250 in royalties. The book was originally called *The American Radical Movement, 1918-1940.* The title was changed in galley proof by my editor to *The Radical Failure.* It did surprisingly well—thanks in part to an absurd review in *Time* which described it as a Maoist critique of American politics.

I am now writing another book, also a true reading of history. *Time* take note. My working title is *The American Liberal Tradition between the Wars,* carefully avoiding the use of dates which my editor says is death. But may I assume that most readers will know *which* wars? My wife, Tammi, thinks not. She has an alternative title. It is *Son of Failure.*

Her wry humor is inspired by the fact that I am not presently working on the manuscript. It lies before me in messy piles. She asks me occasionally if I want her to dust it. Detesting sentiment, we show concern for each other with ironies. It's a talent we share.

I am not working on *The American Liberal Tradition between the Wars* because I find it dull. Worse, I am no longer sure of my political stance. *The Radical Failure* was a lament. I was solid on the left. My colleagues still introduce me as "our radical," smiling to indicate that for all my irascibility, for all my outspoken disgust with our capitalist system and our C students, I'm really no threat. Not at my age. My students, harsher still, write me off as a mere liberal. And my daughter, Hildy, who is eleven, tells me that I am reincarnated from a medieval prince who died young looking for the "magic grail."

Or perhaps I have stopped working on *The American Liberal Tradition between the Wars* merely because something else has caught my attention. My concentration isn't what it used to be. My concerns shift like the wind. In the past two weeks, for example, I have been reading and rereading my father's journals. I tried going through them when I was twenty—he being ten years dead then and my mother nine years gone. That seemed like long enough to wait. The books covered the years 1919 to 1938, the year of his death. They were already history. I had just come through the Second World

War and anything pre-Munich was already history. Was safe. Or so I thought.

I tried to read them objectively. I was majoring in history then, concentrating on the impact of Hegel and Marx. My father had been a real estate investor, a manipulator of working men's lives. He was a strike-breaker (the Boston Police strike), a block-buster (slum property) and a ferocious anti-Semite. Like most parents, he was inexcusable. So I went at his journals with historical detachment. Good primary source material, I said to myself.

But it didn't turn out that way. I began to feel like a voyeur. I read spasmodically, in hot flashes. And I reformed periodically, slamming the books back in the shoe boxes where they were stored. Finally, I gave up. They were not, I decided, good primary source material.

But here they are again. Like seeds, they have germinated. The shoe boxes have been replaced with a sturdy liquor carton with "Napoleon Brandy" printed on the sides. Beneath the label is a silhouette of its namesake. Appropriate.

Here in my study with the marsh view I begin once again with February, 1919. That was when his first wife died. She died of the flu. Even the very rich died of the flu in 1919.

She had given my father two children, my half-brother and half-sister. There was a third child within her. The infant was buried *in utero*. They would make an interesting archeological find, child in parent—assuming one maintained historical objectivity.

These little books are visually more like diaries than journals. This particular volume is faded blue. It was once locked with a clasp. I broke that years ago. The book naturally falls open to early February, 1919. This may be because I have studied that page a good deal, or perhaps it is only because that is where he pasted the newspaper ad. It is from the *Boston Herald*. It is beginning to turn yellow, but it is entirely legible. It reads as follows.

Help Wanted—Female
Housekeeping governess of extraordinary qualifications
wanted by widower to manage house and two children,

age 4 and 7 years, who will be primarily cared for by nurse maid; age between 25 and 35 preferred; must be lady completely at ease in any society, passionately devoted to children and competent to plan and oversee their care when they are well or sick, and competent to run so easily a house where four maids are kept as to consider that work incidental; must be able to buy children's clothes with perfect taste, buy house supplies of all kinds and order all house repairs, etc. Must be in vigorous health and have a disposition that is invariably sunny, responsive and spontaneous; must be fond of romping with children out of doors and able to teach them simple subjects; must be nominally a Protestant, but not too religious; must be logical and preferably intellectual. No limit as to the possible salary to the right person. This is a very exceptional opportunity for a very exceptional lady.

I have read this perhaps fifty times. It still gives me a shiver. A cluster of chromosomes is sending out signals through the *Boston Herald*. It is calling for another set. It is specifying type, size, composition. I am witnessing the very first arrangement of factors which will, eventually, produce me. I know this because I have read ahead. Guiltily, I observe my own conception.

Meanwhile there are the dead to bury. A member of the family, I help with the burial—page by page.

Feb. 21, 1919. Funeral at noon by Dr. Howe who married us. Was in Church of Our Savior, same as our wedding.

Feb. 22, 1919. Took children to Croftham by train with Marguerite and Harriette, nurses. Fondsworths joined us at my request. February thaw. Light easterlies. Bay is a pale blue. Went for long walks along coast. Breaks my heart to think how Leona would have loved it.

Voyeurs must be patient. Hours pass with no rewards. In this case, the management of his household and his business affairs make me restless. I tell myself that as a historian I am learning something about the economic and political biases of the day, that it is all important, that I have a perfect right to spend my time this way. I am getting to know him.

For business, he managed the Boston branch of Imbrie and Co., an investment company which was already making inroads on South America and had its eye on Europe, a corporate empire on the move. He also had his own firm, Gordon Means, Inc., which was named not for himself, not for his father, but for his grandfather by the same name. This in America!

For pleasure he had a summer home in Croftham, just south of Cape Cod. It was two hours from Boston. His father had built the place and shaped the coastline to fit his needs. He enjoyed designing seawalls, jetties, and channels. He—my grandfather this is—liked to do things on a broad scale. Coal for spring and fall heating was trimmed in his own mill. Iceboxes were the walk-in type, tall enough to hang a steer. He was a small man with a merry smile. Like my father, he had a special knack with slum property.

By 1919, all the building had been completed—nearby homes for my Great Uncle Frederick and Uncle Clarendon, tennis courts, stables, boathouses, and an eight-hole golf course. There was nothing left to do but play at sports and plant things. My father was forever planting things at Croftham. Skipping ahead, looking for that governess, I am tangled with his horticulture.

March 28, Sat., 1919. Took children and nurses and one cook down to Croftham on train. Will spend a week. Worth commuting by train when weather is good. First day was raw. Wind and a little sleet. Managed to clear winter damage in pine grove. Uncovered rose bushes and removed burlap windguards from around rhododendrons.

March 29, Sun., 1919. Warm again. Forsythia starting out. All kinds of birds in profusion. But the beauty of it depresses me too. Can't help thinking of how Leona would have loved it. I cover it up in forced geniality and much activity—mulching rose beds, clearing dead wood, pruning apple trees and grape vines. Children spend much time with the pony.

March 30, Mon., 1919. Commute to Boston. Children in hands of Miss Winslow. She is turning out to be fine. Children take to her tremendously.

There she is! Miss Hilda Winslow, housekeeping governess, winner of twenty-five applicants.

She was a country girl. Raised in a small town on Cape Cod I'll call Burnham. A tall, lanky girl. At fourteen she was driving the school barge (a long, open, two-horse wagon) and having to discipline the cut-ups and wiseacres. Had trouble until her father taught her to use a fifteen-foot bullwhip accurately enough to flip off buttons. No trouble after that.

She was a good Baptist girl. She had never danced, played cards, sipped wine, or touched a boy. She knew that the seeds of a tomato would kill you, and she knew from experience how many hours it took picking them out with tweezers. She also knew that the devil existed in visible form, crouching in the wood closet or under the bed, ready to touch your thigh with his long, scaly finger.

She had been baptized in the sea, townspeople on the beach singing, some wailing. It was a ceremony which, if repeated on the same beach today, would bring the police.

She took off for the city as soon as she could. So did four out of five in that family. The only one left was insane. In Boston, she went to nursing school. Flu epidemic made a farce out of training program. Everyone too busy taking care of the dead. Bodies lined up in the hallways. Main problem was to keep the rats from getting at them before someone took them off to wherever they went. Hilda Winslow's training consisted of guarding corpses in the corridors, midnight to ten in the morning. They armed her with a poker. To hell with nursing.

Then a job as "companion" to an elderly bulldog of a Bostonian woman. We'll call her Mrs. Jamieson to avoid waking the dead. Mrs. Jamieson needed help to fight off creeping senility. Insisted that her companion study for and receive a chauffeur's license—this including the skills of changing a tire (pry casing off rim with a wrecking bar; patch puncture; work tube and casing back on; pump up to pressure; allow one hour working time), also changing oil, greasing, removing and cleaning plugs, etc. Drove Mrs. Jamieson out West in 1918. Was the first driver to make it up to the top of Pike's Peak that spring. May have been the first woman driver to do same in any season. Took great pleasure in driving. Detested Mrs. Jamieson.

Somewhere I saw a photo of Hilda Winslow at the wheel. Tall, straight-backed, long hands, long fingers curled around the wheel, a Roman nose, large and dark eyes. She could have been a Vogue model in period costume.

She hadn't discovered her beauty yet. The nurses didn't notice. The corpses didn't speak. And Mrs. Jamieson kept it a secret. Companions are hard to find. So Hilda still thought she was an awkward, too-tall country girl. But beneath those layers of Baptist repression there were needs which startled her.

"When I first worked for your father," she told me years later, "I was a very lonely young girl. I can remember going down to Filene's bargain basement just to brush against people."

When she told me this, she was dying of cancer. She had been a widow for a year. The nursing home was filled with much older people. Again she was lonely. Wistfully, she told me that there were only two experiences she would like to have once more: eating lobster thermidor and having sexual intercourse. Neither was possible at that stage.

At that point for her, everything was running out. But that's not my concern here. Back in 1919 the tide for her was on the flood. She had never slept with a man or tasted lobster thermidor. They were sweeping toward her.

April 19, Sat. 1919. Planned weekend in Croftham, but Gordy has a cold. Miss Winslow and I took Dulce to Franklin Park Zoo then to Arnold Arboretum which except for the sea is my favorite spot. Great profusion of budding and blossoming apple, dogwood, pear trees etc.

In evening Miss Winslow and I took Dulce to see Fred Stone in "Jack O Lantern." Wonderful show, especially for children. Dulce's first play. She was ecstatic. Will never forget her expression of amazement when the curtain went up.

April 20, Sunday, 1919. Gordy's cold is better. Bundled him up and took him and Dulce to aquarium in Motor with Miss W. Then over by ferry to East Boston and around home through Charlestown, etc. Took time off to inspect tenements of Dwelling House Associates. New policy is to buy and sell in units of three or more to save legal fees.

In evening played Vivaldi selections on violin with Miss W. as appreciative audience.

I remember that violin. It was a richly golden brown, almost a living thing. And the case was dark blue. It was about the same shade and degree of wear as the diary I now study. The violin went in the case at the end of the day and the two latches snapped shut. They were brass and pitted, like the clasp of the diaries which some twenty years ago I pried open with a screwdriver. Strange that I could do that prying open but couldn't stand reading them. Perhaps the difference is that I am forty-five now. I know more. Or I'm supposed to. It's getting to be that time. When he was my age, he had only seven years to live. I wonder if he saw patterns? "What did you see?" I ask aloud. He fails to answer. I listen to the sea breeze whisper by the dormer eaves, and from downstairs comes the sound of Hildy playing scales on the recorder.

She is talented at that. She plays with an adult group of recorder enthusiasts during the winter. My boys are also musically talented. Weldon, an extrovert at thirteen, plays the trumpet and improvises with abandon. Pete, my namesake, is two years older and has an eighteenth-century restraint to him. The clarinet is his instrument. I don't know where they get all this talent and interest. I have never had time for music and I don't go about lamenting the fact. History is my subject. I don't spread myself thin.

Yet as I listen to the wind and the sound of Hildy's playing, I feel an odd sense of lament, of longing. Felt the same a week ago on listening to the three of them adapt a Mozart quartet. I had to confess —privately—that I am capable of envy. And love.

I look at the cover of the diary again, fingering its dry, cracked surface. It reminds me of the blue tie-print kerchief which he kept in the case and placed under his chin when he played. I remember the kerchief against his chin, the fleshiness of his cheek, the beads of sweat which would accumulate, the slight blue tinge of what had been shaved hours earlier. This is vivid because I had to endure his damn musicals—my father and three or four friends playing, all formally attired, and perhaps four others as "audience," sipping cordials. Nothing for me to do but to study the pattern of the kerchief against his chin, the fleshiness of his cheek, the beads of sweat which would accumulate, and the slight blue tinge of what he had shaved hours earlier. I used to wonder even then why I hated him so.

April 21, Mon., 1919. Spent heavy day at work, dividing time between the two offices. Work a blessing since without it I get despondent. Occasionally have a good cry when alone, but it is better to stay with people. In evenings, Miss W. is a great comfort. But tonight she is off. Studied Industrial Chemistry (re. Georgia creosote plant) and tried more of the Brazil book (re. Rio holdings). Prefer to read it out loud to Miss W.

April 23, Wed., 1919. Played squash at noon today and broke tendon. Had to hop to taxi and home to bed. Furious.

April 24, Thur., 1919. Bed all day. Considerable pain. In terrible mood because work pending at both offices. Only consolation is that Miss W. is a wonderful nurse. Is patient, thoughtful, sweet and en-

tertaining. Being in bed where Leona died adds to my daily heart-
aches and sorrow. Spend a good deal of time reviewing her last
moments and days.

Had nice call from Mr. Manning. Miss W. a good masseur and
manicure, etc. Most efficient and sweet. We are reading Brazil
history etc. together and I work on Industrial Chemistry alone.

April 25, Fri. 1919. Still in bed. Day of big parade of 26th Division
just returned from France. I saw some formation etc. out Marlboro
St. window, but not the full parade. Children went to Gen Edward's
house on Commonwealth Ave. with Miss W. Bill Edward is Com-
mander of DW. Parade route designed to pass his place because he
has gout.

Bitter cold. Snow flurries with gale. Several sea planes flying
around. One crashed in the bay. Damn fool.

April 27, Sunday, 1919. Beautiful glorious day. Children to their
grandparents for day. I worked for a while on the Brooklyn Corp.
papers and on Dwelling House Associates holdings. Miss W. is a
treasure as a companion. She is completely unselfconscious, and of
absolutely even and sweet disposition. Has a tremendous amount of
character and ability. Always cheerful and helpful.

Was she really? Can anyone be? Can I trust his memory? Can I
trust my own? Sitting here in my study, looking out my dormer window across salt marshes, I try to catch memories of my own. There
are so few. Her face, long, lean, leathered, animated in argument.
Every meal was a lively argument—political or economic. Or her
face again—no, just her eyes, made slightly rounder as if she were
holding them open by an act of will. This after the third martini.
Without fail. Or her hands on the driving wheel, long fingers curled
firmly, competently.

But this is no good as an album. Whoever took a closeup of his
parent's hand on a driving wheel? What kind of a momento is that?
Why do I spend time up here, half seeing the gulls wheel over the
marshes, half dreaming? I recall my wife's comment at

breakfast: "It's insane." How easy it is to use that phrase these days. Still, I don't have the strength to refute her. I shrug. She says, "It's spooky, your burying yourself in that stuff." This in a half-joking tone which is her style. Then, not joking at all: "You worry the hell out of me."

I've worried about her too, on occasion. When Pete was born, for example. There were two days of crisis. My stomach ached with longing. I wanted to hear her voice again. And now she must feel that I am drifting from her just as she did from me then.

And what possesses me? A diary. It would be far less disturbing for everyone if I were involved in some complex love affair.

By May of that year my father apparently felt that things were sufficiently settled at home to take a business trip to New York City. That was where the home office of Imbrie and Co. was. He also liked the theater.

May 17, Sat. 1919. Children with their grandparents for the weekend. Took 8:30 a.m. train to N.Y.C. Lengthy and rewarding conference with jIEMB Re. Imbrie & Co. (BGFL) for lunch and afterward in hotel. Celebrated with claret cup at Henri's. Leisurely dinner at Delmonicos. Excellent cognac and good cheer. Then to Mrs. Fiske in "Miss Nell of N'Orleans" in evening. Arrived late, but no problem since we had box seats. After theatre we went to Hotel Claridge basement for drinks. A most unusual and rewarding sort of evening.

I recall using this as anecdotal material during my twenties and thirties. "It was a completely honest diary," I would say on the basis of leafing through those few entries, "except that, being typically American, he placed his business details in code."

I'm a better historian now. Or at least less impulsive. I worked on the code earlier this spring. That was when I first began to stray from my manuscript on liberalism between the wars. There's something about a code which is more compelling than a chronicle of liberal intention.

It wasn't too hard, really. After all, *jIEMB* has the same number of letters as *Hilda*, his perfect governess and eventually the mother of me and my full sister. It was a simple code—each letter one off from the one intended (spelling *IHDLA*) and then reversed in pairs, *Hilda.* It was only intended to guard against prying servants. And children prematurely curious.

So he was off to New York with his beautiful Hilda, and following the same code I learned that the next phrase, "Re Imbrie & Co." is "FAKE."

A trick. You old bastard. "And was it set for me? Did you know I would go prying? How could you guess? I was only ten when you quit on me. How could you guess when you didn't even know me?"

I must stop talking. Twice this summer Tammi has overheard me. She's worried about schizophrenia. It's in the air these days and highly contagious. Our winter caretaker had to be locked up last December. Tammi thinks the Nova Scotia climate brings it on. She could be right. I haven't been myself lately, and I'm not sure what the alternatives are.

I struggle to maintain my historical objectivity. After all, I am forty-five and he is only thirty-four. That should give me a kind of upper hand, a certain self-assurance. It would be completely irrational of me to think of him as a domineering old tyrant. I am discovering him as a young man about to enter a new adventure. And I'm not entirely sure I approve. After all, what do these two have in common? What will come of it all?

I study his financial activities instead. They suggest hard work and daring. And reliability. I feel safer, somehow. These are not the makings of schizophrenics. I try to visualize him charged with energy and optimism, a kind of Teddy Roosevelt, conducting a "busy day in N.Y.C."

May 19, Mon. 1919. Busy day N.Y.C. Negotiations in a.m. with three firms. Planning session at Imbrie office all afternoon. Dinner

and late-evening session with James Imbrie in his apartment. Discussed new steamship line to Cuba. Future looks good indeed.
May 20, Tue. 1919. Very successfully launched our participation with Blake Bros. in Conn. Mills. 7% Pfd. Tax Free in Mass. @ 98 1/2   Big Rio Issue launched. Twice oversubscribed. $10,000,000 serial 6 1/2% basis. Great success and awakened lively interest. Put in fifteen-hour day & returned to Boston on the midnight train.
May 21, Wed. 1919. Met at South Station in early morning by jIEMB. Headed for Croftham secretly. Enormous picnic breakfast in drizzle somewhere between Milton & Stoughton. Hot kidney pie, etc. Then motored to Croftham. Lunch at Cottage. Light S.W. breeze. Everything very still. Went for walk for three or four miles. Had cozy time back of Bourne's Hill. Then motored to sheep farm. An ideal day.

A word about the "Cottage" at Croftham. It was the first of those three homes. It was a shingled, two-storied affair, rambling and low and an odd assortment of dormers and eaves. There was a little window seat in the nursery which was set into one of those dormers. It overlooked the lawn and the sea. As the youngest in the family, the nursery was mine as long as the place lasted. I would lie there pretending to read. I would watch the waves. Sometimes I would dream that they wouldn't stop at the sea wall. In these dreams I stared with quiet fascination as the waves came up across the lawn, each one clawing its way further than the next. I always woke before the house itself was struck.

Eventually, of course, it was struck. Why should a mere house be immune? It was 1938. My father had died the year before. Just in time. The hurricane which hit New England in 1938 was the first one in anyone's memory. We were unprepared. The sea raked the entire point all night, dumping almost everything into the cove. We had all been evacuated to an old farmhouse inland, but when we walked back the next morning, my childhood had been erased. Wiped clean. The house was gone. The cellar was an indentation in the sand. All the trees were gone. The gardens. Sand and rock covered the point. A moonscape. Here and there we would find a chair, a sink, an iron bedstead half-buried. The land was so foreign that we couldn't locate where the tennis court used to be or the gardens. The cove was a clutter of timbers, shingled walls, trees, parts of boats. In the middle, just showing above the surface, was something identifiable: a section of the roof and the dormer of my room.

Mother died that winter. She refused treatment for cancer. And why not? It was 1939 and she was sure that the Germans would win. They were as invincible as the thrust of a hurricane. "You'll find some way to endure it," she told me from her nursing home bed. "But I just don't have the stomach for it." This was a wry bit of humor considering the type of cancer she had.

But the Germans didn't win. Like the tide, they receded. And the rest of us did endure. I thought it was going to be easy once the war was over, but it hasn't been. Not recently. It has not been easy to endure what we have become. She was right to talk about endurance, but she misunderstood who the enemy would be. Who would have guessed that it would be us?

But it is not politics which keeps me with these journals. If it were, there would be some justification. It is more subtle than that. Too subtle for me to trace. Politics I can argue; but whatever this is, it eludes me, hidden in morning mists. It is no subject for a historian. Bewildered, I slip back to 1919, to the next entry.

May 22, thur. 1919. Woke up to sound of song sparrows. Children are at their grandparents. Have the place to ourselves. After last week's cold snap, we are now having real spring weather. Early morning sea fog burned off by 8:00. The air very still. Sun and sea brilliant. Looked out bedroom window and saw doe and fawn feeding near rose garden. The "big event" now PDTONVBNFUE and "new situation" launched re Imbrie & Co. (BGFL).

Translated, the " 'big event' is now CONSUMMATED" and the reference to Imbrie is "FAKE." I recall sharing dawns with Tammi here in Worwich when we first owned it. Is it possible to recover and repeat such experiences?

May 23, Fri. 1919. Up early again to watch dawn over the bay. Two loons & a number of gulls. Beautiful. Gardens doing well. Practiced tennis and golf with Miss W. She has never played either but is most enthusiastic. Planted more in garden with Miss W. She is a hard worker. We then transplanted some Scotch pines and a couple of Austrians. In the evening we took the blue canoe across to Marsh Harbor. Not a ripple of wind and too early for bugs. Not a single light along the coast. Navigated entirely by star glow. Spent some time in salt hay field at head of Marsh Harbor. PDTONVBNJUOP made PDQNFMFU and FQGSDFU—re. Imbrie & Co. investments (BGFL).

And so in salt hay the "CONSUMMATION" was "made COMPLETE and PERFECT" and as usual the reference to Imbrie is "FAKE."

Marsh Harbor I had forgotten. Surprising, considering how important it was to us when we were young. It drifts back clearly now, fog lifting.

It is a winding inlet working up into the marshland. I've been told that even after half a century the developers have found no way to fill it in and desecrate it. It is closer to being eternal than anything else I know—closer than the home at Croftham, the grounds, the barn, parents.

And now I recall how we as children—the two of us born years after that entry—used to explore its winding canals, paddling our homemade kayaks. We would turn first one way and then the other, mobile as tiny, wriggling fish, working our way upstream, the dank saline smell heavy about us, past soft beds of salt hay.

The tall grasses parted before us, whispering against our kayaks. Occasionally we were startled by the splash of an otter, a vibrato of wings. Enormous crabs scuttled within reach. Once we found a dead gull, decaying; even gulls, we decided, had to die sometime.

Occasionally the channel would open up into a salt pond. I see one now with two herons standing in the exact center, one upright and one inverted in the mirror of the sky.

"The headwaters" were what we said we were seeking. We were thinking of the Nile. Our landscape had none of the sweep or the grandeur of the Nile; no historian had bothered with it. But how beautifully we aproached it—openly, without judgment or preconception. Ours was a blend of fascination and reverence.

I watch this boy in the lead kayak, threading his way through multi-colored grasses, and I see him beckon to me. Startled, I realize this child of eight, this explorer with my name, is reaching out to me, teaching me how to explore the sources before me. He is showing me how to meet my parents.